The First and Last Love

Frieda Shan

I0576021

FRIEDA SHAN &
NICK SACHSENHEIM
EDITIONS

The First and Last Love

© 2025 Frieda Shan

Though this story is rooted in truth, it remains a work of fiction. Names, characters, places, and events are altered, imagined, or combined. Any resemblance to actual persons, living or dead, or to actual events is coincidental.

Published by

FRIEDA SHAN &
NICK SACHSENHEIM
EDITIONS

ISBN 979-8-9931649-0-8
Cover design by 100Covers
Interior design by the author.

There are two loves
That forever change a person
One's first. And one's last.

First love arrives passionately,
Like the heat of your lips
In the sun-drenched deserts
Where only your touch is my oasis.
It stays daringly
Defying all reason, we allow our shadows
To dance on candle lit walls
With our breaths taken away.
But this love passes fleetingly
Like the flicker of a lighter
I allowed my heart to be yours
Yet you only burned scars in mine.

Last love arrives unknowingly
Like a familiar melody in an unheard song
Its touch is patient and tender
An oasis, not just a mirage.
It stays when my heart bleeds
To hold all that cracked open
Until the stitches faded
And pain was only a memory.

Last love holds a lifetime
No longer in the shadows
It holds all that I am
And dreams of all that we've become.

L.W.S.
@heart_of_forget_me_not

Author's Note

This story is rooted in truth, not in the details, but in the feeling. The kind of truth you carry quietly for years, folded into memory, reshaped by time.

It's a story about first love, the kind that catches you off guard, rewires something inside you, and leaves a mark that never fully fades. But it's also a story about clarity. About learning the difference between being wanted and being seen. Between secrecy and trust. Between the love that pulls you under and the love that walks beside you.

Some loves don't last—but they leave us changed. And if we're lucky, the stories they give us teach us how to recognize the love that will.

Thank you for reading mine.

—Frieda Shan

Introduction

I consider myself a very lucky woman. I was deeply loved twice—by my first and by my last love.

When I met Marc, I thought I had been loved before. I thought I had been in love before. I was wrong. What I had known was affection. Attachment. Even desire, but not this. Not the kind of love that sears itself into your memory so fiercely that decades later, a single song, a certain scent, the scrape of a lighter—and you're back there.

It was the summer of 1998. A summer that gave me everything. And then took it all away.

That summer taught me what love could be. How intoxicating. How tender. How all-consuming. And how dangerous. It didn't just break my heart. It broke something deeper, something I hadn't even known was fragile.

It nearly destroyed me. And yet, I wouldn't trade it. Because it also prepared me for what would come after. The man who would become my last love. The one who knew me not as a girl in the middle of her first rebellion, but as a woman who had already walked through fire.

This is the story of that one summer.

Of Marc.

Of me.

Of love, and loss, and how some things—no matter how far you run, or how much time passes—never quite leave you.

So if you're ready, I'll tell you. About the first and the last loves of my life.

CHAPTER 1

The Place That Chose Me

February 1997. I'm twenty-five, leaving the safety of the capital behind. Everyone else calls it reckless. I call it freedom —and in the end, Kuwait feels less like a choice than a place that chose me. I could have picked easier postings, more relaxing ones. But I wanted heat. Distance. A country still marked by war yet alive with possibility. At the Foreign Office, postings appear like invitations on the intranet —destinations that can reshape a life if you say yes. When Kuwait came up, I did.

Now, with one suitcase, one assignment, and a plane ticket in hand, I'm ready to embark on a new journey. The departure hall of the airport in the capital of my home country smells faintly of melting snow and stale coffee. Outside, winter still clings to the streets, but my mind is already drifting to visions of coastal, sand-veiled skylines, sunlit streets, and the sensation of sea air on my skin. I've grown weary of harsh winters and endless dark evenings. I long for warmth, for the taste of saltwater. I yearn for a fresh start. Though I don't realize it yet, this assignment will transform me, creating a distinct before and after. For now, I'm simply a young woman boarding a plane—free, open to possibilities, and quietly certain that time is on my side.

Diplomacy feels like home to me, with its formalities, unspoken rules, and the waypoints of international life. My father's career as a diplomat meant my childhood unfolded from one embassy to the next, watching the world through embassy windows. So when the Kuwait assignment came up, it felt like fate, a familiar rhythm drawing me back. However, beneath the structure and ceremony lies the pain of constant goodbyes—new cities, new schools, friendships that never fully take root. Just as I start to understand the language, the rhythm, and the rules of a place, it's time to move on. Again.

I'm adept at letting go, skilled in the art of starting anew. It teaches resilience, certainly, but also leaves me with a subtle sense of dislocation, a grief that doesn't shout but accumulates over time. While I never doubt the lifestyle itself, I have yet to recognize the quiet burden it places on me.

Beginning a new life feels like walking through a door into the unknown. And I wonder who I'll be when I return. Married? To whom? Or perhaps still single. The globe seems vast, uncharted, brimming with possibilities I've never dared to imagine. That thought thrills me: at my age, in this new place, almost anything feels within reach.

As I step off the plane in Kuwait City, the desert air strikes me—dry, warm, oddly purifying. Kuwait feels hushed compared to my memories. I left during Iraq's 1990 invasion under circumstances I rarely discuss. Now, seven years on, I'm eager to see what's changed. Underneath it all, though—the broad roads, beige-and-white buildings, the hush between them, and the dull roar of air conditioning—everything feels exactly the same.

Kuwait speaks in many tongues. Arabic, Urdu, Tagalog, English, Bengali—voices that mingle on the streets like layers of dust. What holds this small nation together is labor: millions of hands from every corner of the world, building, cleaning, driving, serving. The languages don't unite so much as overlap, stitched loosely together by necessity. And yet, that patchwork is what makes Kuwait so endlessly fascinating, a country where the world gathers, colliding and coexisting in one unlikely place.

The country moves—constantly. The rhythm of migration seeps into everything, shaping how we arrive, how leave, and how we learn to stay. The highways never rest. Day or night, they rumble with traffic—massive gas-guzzlers and smaller, sand-speckled cars like my own. It's as if the entire country is perpetually in transit, even if everyone's only en route to a mall or a mosque.

Over the next couple of weeks, I settle into the routine of my new post. I report each morning to the embassy, a two-story building, its walls colored in a sun-bleached white, dulled by decades of heat and dust. My job is to stamp visas, review passport renewal documents, and answer questions from Kuwaitis and expats hoping to travel. On my first day, my boss, a genial man in his early fifties with a knack for re-membering small details, introduces me to colleagues over coffee in the chancery kitchen. These are the connections— fellow diplomats, a few local hires from India and Sri Lanka —that form the loose net of my early days.

My new home is a small but cozy apartment on the em-bassy building's second floor, filled with colorful and beloved items from home. The vibrant blue sofa and sunny yellow armchair I shipped over stand out against the tiled floor, while the shelves of beloved books add a personal touch. The sprawling balcony, although mostly useless in the heat, pro-vides a view of the surrounding area and a tiny glimpse of the coast in the distance, where the desert meets the Gulf.

Like most Western women here, I don't take public transit. The heat alone makes it unbearable, but more than that, Kuwait runs on a rigid social hierarchy. Not everyone is even permitted to hold a driver's license—it depends on your in-come, your nationality, your job. Buses and shared taxis are left to those at the bottom of the ladder. So I buy my first car —a dark-blue Suzuki Swift with beige diplomatic plates— giving me freedom, or at least the illusion of it. In reality, my choices are limited: the demilitarized zone to the north is off-limits, Iran to the northeast feels unwelcoming to non-Mus-

3

lims, and Saudi Arabia to the south and west is closed to single women traveling alone. I never questioned it then; I accepted the limits as if they are simply part of the landscape.

As summer edges closer, the temperatures soar above 115°F every day. No one strolls the waterfront; instead, cars stream to the malls, the only places where air-conditioning can make you forget the desert outside. I move with the flow. Sometimes I meet friends at one of the glamorous shopping malls; more often, I shop alone. Hotel beach clubs and pools offer a different kind of escape, but their steep prices make them rare indulgences.

My days fall into sequence: stamped visas, evening receptions, and a modest circle of friends—Poles, Germans, a few Kuwaitis—people who, like me, are carving out a life in this suspended world. I am learning, slowly, how to endure the heat: retreat indoors, find company where we can, and let routine soften the edges of isolation.

Among my circle is an elderly German couple I meet at one of the embassy's informal gatherings. They become like surrogate parents, inviting me for dinners and weekend excursions. They introduce me to the city's best *shawarma* with garlic sauce and guide me through souks selling oddities. On one outing, we encounter a tiny plastic statue hidden among baskets and kitchenware: a naked boy wearing only a red cap, his smile fixed and mischievous. My friends pick it up and gingerly pull a lever. Suddenly, a thin stream of water arcs across the counter, drenching a row of bright yellow tea towels.

We stand frozen for a moment, then dissolve into uncontrollable laughter—tears streaming, a guffaw you can't stifle, even if it feels wildly inappropriate. A peeing boy in a land where even bare elbows invite stares! It's absurd, scandalous, and utterly perfect. The vendor chuckles with us; he's probably seen it before. Maybe absurdity is a universal dialect.

I can't imagine who would buy something like this—except us. In that moment, formalities vanish. We're not colleagues, not tied to diplomatic ranks, just three people undone by something so silly it becomes liberating.

My social life widens when I befriend Ania, a spirited Polish woman I meet through embassy contacts. She and her Kuwaiti boyfriend, Badr, invite me to their house often, to barbecue or hang out, and over time they become close friends. They also bring me to Wednesday-night parties, ushering in the start of the weekend. These are clandestine gatherings whispered about hours before they start. They unfold in sprawling mansions behind white walls so high they feel more like declarations: What happens here stays here. Armed guards vet guests against an unrecorded list. There's plenty of smuggled alcohol, expensive, illicit, always in demand. A bottle of whiskey can run eighty to a hundred dollars, but hosts spare no expense, and they know where to find it.

Inside, in the dimly lit room, Kuwaiti men of all ages intertwine with expat women, mostly Filipino hostesses or manicurists, sometimes in more precarious roles. I loathe watching them; I feel pity, even shame. One night, I sit at the bar with Ania: she, nursing a glass of whiskey, me, sipping a cold beer. Badr is absent, spending the evening with his would-be Kuwaiti fiancée, and I can't help but wonder why Ania stays, why any of them do. She's said it before: It's not the money, not really, and not the stories she tells her parents in Gdansk about saving to raise her daughter, but the way a Kuwaiti man will stare at her, hungry, or the way she moves through this city invisible until she's not. However, as I can personally attest, Ania and Badr truly love each other. The true tragedy here is that Badr is bound by family honor and tradition and therefore must marry a Kuwaiti girl.

So Wednesday after Wednesday, we watch the parade of men. They arrive in pairs or trios, pressed *dishdashas*, the traditional long white robes of men here, crisp, gold watches catching the light, a faint trail of *oud* with its dark and smoky fragrance, following them. When they lower themselves beside the Filipino women, the exchange is silent but unmistakable—measured in glances, refills, and the slow drama of who lights whose cigarette. The longer I watch, the more I despise being a spectator to it.

I eventually stop going, not out of fear, but because the emptiness repels me. One night in particular, the image of a hostess laughing too loudly under a stranger's gaze stays with me for days. It's not the transactions in plain sight; it's the way the whole scene feels uncomfortably close to what I imagine a brothel must be.

But it's another reminder that here, when it is love, it must be clandestine. Tender, loyal, real feelings confined to parallel lives—separate homes, separate stories. All of us learning to vanish in our own ways.

A few months later, I come across an article in the local English-language newspaper reporting that one of the hosts had their party broken up by Kuwaiti security forces. The event was halted, guests were detained, and the mansion was thoroughly searched under glaring fluorescent lights. The repercussions for expats are immediate and severe: imprisonment followed by deportation. In contrast, Kuwaitis might receive fines or warnings. I feel relieved that I left when I did—not fortunate, but wise. I sensed the danger, noticed the change in atmosphere, and trusted my instincts. For once, I prioritized caution over curiosity, and it spared me.

I slip into a peculiar solitude. It's not loneliness, but something more diffuse. A weightless rhythm that keeps me near the surface of things. I'm not unhappy. Just... not anchored. There's a quiet thrum under it all, like my body knows change is coming before I do.

Even my apartment feels suspended, functional, but not quite mine yet. The air-conditioning jumps to life at odd intervals—loud, abrupt, mechanical. It startles me at first. Later, I barely notice. It's always like that when you start somewhere new: the quirks stand out until they don't. Until they become the background noise of a life you're slowly learning to inhabit.

As summer drags on with its blistering heat—more than seven months since I first arrived—the world outside mirrors something inside me: slow, heavy, suspended. I move with it: slow mornings at the embassy, still afternoons behind heavy drapes. My movements outside are rationed with calculated trips to the corner shop basics, short drives to more fully stocked grocery stores at dusk when the air lets me breathe again.

Then the dust storms arrive. Without warning, the wind picks up, groaning until it feels like the earth is fracturing. Sheets of grit sweep in from Iraq and Saudi Arabia, blotting out the sky. The sun becomes a pale, distant idea behind a thick, yellowish veil. Everything turns the color of old parchment. Edges disappear.

Indoors, a fine layer of dust settles on counters, closets, even the open book by my bedside. I run my finger across the dresser. Dust collects under my nail. I don't bother wiping it off. Outside, it grows so dark you expect rain, but there's no cloud in sight—just endless, clinging dust. It's unsettling, but I'm awed by the spectacle.

No two storms are alike: some skies blaze orange and electric, others drift a muted yellow, as if light itself has grown stale. Even the palm fronds press against the wind, gray with grit. Some storms pass quickly. Others stretch on for days, sealing the city in stillness and sand. I'm grateful for glass and walls. I only dash out for groceries, clipping between doorways and trying to holding my breath until I'm back inside. The storm is relentless yet unforgettable. Then, as suddenly, the dust clears, the sun blazes once more, and with it my smile returns because I'm tired of being stuck inside.

By late summer, humidity climbs, its sticky, suffocating heat driving me indoors once again. Water beads on the windows; the air feels heavy enough to drown in. One night, the power cuts out. Just for a minute. Long enough to feel the desert pressing through the flimsy windows. And when the power comes back, you breathe a sigh of relief.

But when October rolls around and the humidity finally breaks, I breathe deeply. I switch off the air-conditioning, fling open the windows at night, and feel comfort slip back into my bones. The drama of the heavy summer heat fades, and with it, the faint stirring I hadn't realized had settled inside me.

Life settles into a quiet cadence: workdays, evenings at home, small rituals that stave off solitude. I'm grateful for my

German surrogate family—shared dinners, beer, wine, long talks. We trade tiny comforts against the absurdity of this place, especially its sense of impermanence and things left unsaid.

There are nights when I sense the ground shifting, ever so slightly, not from storms, but from something subtler. A current moving beneath the surface. I don't know it yet, but something—someone—is already on his way.

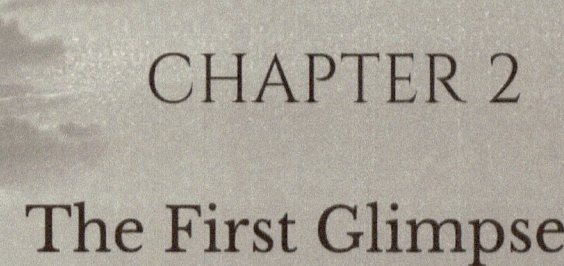

CHAPTER 2

The First Glimpse

After the Gulf War ended in 1991, the United Nations established the Iraq–Kuwait Observer Mission to monitor the fragile ceasefire and patrol the demilitarized zone, or DMZ, between the two countries. Every few months, the mission's soldiers rotate out, replaced by a fresh contingent from the contributing nations. As part of my country's diplomatic presence, I am always invited to the handover ceremonies, when our outgoing military detachment returns home and a fresh unit takes its place—formal yet human rituals where soldiers in desert uniforms salute, flags shift hands, and those who stood watch went home to their families. It is one of the few occasions when the worlds of the embassy and the military truly overlap.

In Kuwait, loneliness can cling like the desert heat. Among the expat community, there is a quiet ache—men and women far from home, hemmed in by strict rules, an unfamiliar culture, and the knowledge that their time here is often measured in months. Perhaps that's why I make a point of greeting the expats and the military officers from our country with genuine warmth. It's my own small act of diplomacy, a way of softening the edges for those defending freedom under the UN's watch. Some might imagine ulterior motives, but they'd be wrong. My mother taught me that hospitality is both a duty and a gift, and in this place, it feels like a calling.

I can still picture the moment I first lay eyes on him. It's early October 1997, the heat still pressing down, when I set out for the demilitarized zone. The drive feels ceremonial in itself with the bustling freeways of Kuwait City giving way to a narrow ribbon of highway stretching north into nothing. On either side: pale sand, the shimmer of heat, the occasional caravan of camels moving like a mirage. Checkpoints break the monotony. Armed, uniformed guards lean in to examine IDs, the sun sharp on their pressed uniforms. By the time I reach the military camp—ringed with HESCO barriers (those giant wire-mesh crates filled with sand), barbed wire, and watchtowers—it feels as though I've crossed a border into a world that belongs to everyone and no one at once.

There's a comforting cadence to these ceremonies: crisp salutes, flags snapping in the wind, brisk handshakes, brief greetings, and hushed farewells. The event is formal without being rigid, the sort of gathering where protocol and personal pride coexist. I'm always struck by the significance of watching our officers head out to that slim corridor of desert wedged between two wary nations. It's more than pageantry; it matters. I wear my national dress not as a spectacle, but as a quiet homage to my roots. It simply feels right.

He's part of the incoming unit, but at first he's just another uniform in a sea of them. I'm caught up in farewells, laughing with the men heading home, promising to send photos, raising a paper cup of wine in their honor. New faces blur past without landing. If I notice him at all, it's only in passing —a tall figure standing a little apart, listening more than speaking, his eyes scanning the crowd.

It will be weeks before we speak. Months before I understand what this moment truly was: the first frame in a reel I will play and replay for the rest of my life.

In early 1998, our paths cross again at a lively gathering hosted by my boss in his spacious, warmly lit living room. The air is filled with the hum of animated chatter and bursts of laughter as people move from the kitchen to the living room, balancing plates of hors d'oeuvres. He stands out among the crowd, his tall frame clad in slacks and a simple polo shirt, surrounded by colleagues in an easy conversation. His presence is commanding yet approachable, drawing people in with ease.

He steps forward, hand extended, smile warm enough to crinkle the corners of his eyes.

"Marc," he says. "Captain Marc. We met briefly when I rotated in back in October." He gestures to the man beside him. "This is René, also a captain. He works near headquarters, while my observation post is farther out, deep in the desert, on the Iraqi side of the demilitarized zone."

I take his hand, a small current running through the contact. "Frieda," I say. "I work at the embassy."

We trade a few lines, our words flowing easily as we stand by the bar. René grins. "We usually stick together when we're both in the city. Days off are better with company." Marc tilts his head in agreement, his eyes never quite leaving mine.

Someone suggests tequila, and we lean into the bar, the crowd giving way just enough for us to slip into place at the counter. Glasses are poured, salt passed down the line. We clink, toss them back, and feel the fiery heat trail into our chests. That's all. And yet, there's a quiet ease between us—unforced, natural—like old friends slipping back into a rhythm they'd forgotten.

At some point during the evening, I casually propose lunch, nothing fancy, just a simple meal at my place. They agree without hesitation, and when the weekend arrives, they come. We gather around my modest dining table, which is now set with comforting dishes: slices of roast chicken seasoned with thyme and garlic, buttered baby potatoes, a refreshing cucumber-dill salad, and a basket of freshly baked rolls still warm from the oven. The scent of browned butter and herbs fills the air, blending gently with the soft, cool breeze from the air conditioner, which hums more out of habit than necessity in Kuwait's brief, early-spring warmth.

René leans back a bit and gestures toward the plate. "This is dangerous. You're going to spoil us."

I laugh. "Don't get used to it. It's a one-time diplomatic gesture."

Marc smiles, not looking up. "I'll remember that."

The room is filled with the quiet sounds of cutlery on porcelain, chairs gently moving on the tile floor, and a few half-told stories shared between bites. It's nothing out of the ordinary. Just a meal. But the pace is leisurely. Comfortable. Nothing significant is said, yet the silence settles between us like an old friend. Natural. Not quite a change, but something begins to root itself.

After lunch, none of us is ready to call it a day. Someone suggests we go ice-skating—an absurd idea in the middle of the desert, which is exactly why it appeals. We pile into my car, the doors releasing a wave of heat as we slide inside. The drive across the city is bright and blinding, the air outside shimmering on the asphalt. By the time we step into the covered, air-conditioned rink, the sudden chill carries an unreal quality, a small pocket of winter hidden in the middle of the desert. As I step onto the smooth, glassy surface, I wobble and flail, my arms pinwheeling in a desperate attempt to maintain balance; I'm certainly no natural. Anyone who knows me would confidently wager that I'm more suited to skis over skates; at least skis have the decency to go in a straight line. Marc watches with amusement, bursting into laughter the first time I nearly face-plant onto the hard, cold ice. René glides by with effortless grace, looking back over his shoulder with a playful smirk. Extending his hand toward me, Marc offers steady support. His touch is light and teasing, and his eyes sparkle with a mischievous glint, as if he's been predicting this exact moment ever since the drive to the rink.

Later, back at my apartment, Marc unfurls a backgammon board across the polished surface of the coffee table. The room is softly lit by the setting sun, casting a warm glow over us as we settle onto the plush, inviting cushions of the blue sofa, each cradling a fresh drink in hand. Nearby, René reclines leisurely in the yellow armchair, casually flipping through the glossy pages of a magazine, his eyes occasionally flitting toward us with a hint of mild curiosity.

As Marc guides me through the intricacies of the game, his fingertips gently brush against mine while positioning the checkers, sending a thrilling tremor coursing through me that I strive to ignore. It's the first game we play together—but not the last. Before long, it will become our quiet thread, stitched through nights and weekends, as familiar as the blue sofa.

At some point, he reaches for his glass and I notice the gold band on his left hand. It must have been there earlier, but I hadn't looked for it.

"Married?" I ask, keeping my tone light.

He inclines his head. "A few months ago…"

"She's not here with you?"

His gaze drops briefly. "No. She's back home."

I take this in quietly, listening, filing the detail away without judgment.

The late afternoon light filters softly through the curtains, and for a time it's the three of us—ordinary friends spending an unhurried weekend day together. I enjoy their company, the unpretentious pleasure of cold drinks, simple conversation, the luxury of nowhere else to be. I have no inkling how swiftly things will shift, how innocence will give way to something undeniable. But at that moment it's just lunch, just skating, just a board game.

A few days later, Marc calls to let me know he's in Kuwait City again. When we decide to have dinner together, it's as easy as slipping into a well-worn pair of shoes. Both of us hail from the same country, expatriates stationed in this dry, vigilant city where the sun relentlessly bakes the earth. Here, forming true connections is like finding an oasis, and trusting those connections is even more elusive. Yet, there's a soothing familiarity in sitting across from someone who mirrors your accent, someone who gets your jokes without explanation.

We clink glasses filled with rich red wine, the clatter of cutlery mingling with our laughter. Since Kuwait's strict laws mean alcohol is off the menu in public, dinners always unfold in the privacy of someone's home, where the air is thick with shared stories and the scent of home-cooked meals.

I don't remember where we ate—most likely at my place. I would've cooked something simple, something that could handle red wine and a few cold beers. I remember feeling relaxed. I remember laughing. I remember thinking: He's easy to be around.

And I remember the ring—the quiet fact of it—catching the light as he reached for his glass. He never hid it, never softened the truth. I never thought of disrespecting it. There was no undercurrent, no game. We talked like colleagues. Or neighbors. Or maybe like two people too grown-up, or too careful, to drift past boundaries that weren't theirs to cross.

Away from the office, my personal life seems uncompli-cated—or so I believe. That changed in mid-1997, when I be-gan a long-distance relationship with a man from my home country. We saw each other only sporadically, our conversa-tions carried mostly by letters and costly phone calls. It is more companionship than passion, yet it currently lingers in the background, a thread I haven't decided to cut, but soon will.

One day in mid-February 1998, the man I'm about to leave calls with an unexpected suggestion: meet in South Korea. I hesitate—is it wise to spend ten days with a man you've al-ready decided to break up with? But South Korea strikes me as worth the trip, and maybe it's as good a place as any to mark an ending.

From Kuwait, I fly east. We both know this will be our last time together as a couple, but that doesn't stop us from mak-ing the most of it by exploring Seoul's neon-lit streets, stand-ing in the chill at the bleak demilitarized zone separating North and South Korea, skiing crisp slopes in the middle of the country. The goodbye is polite: he hands my bag to the taxi driver outside the hotel, and I wave from the back seat as the cab pulls into traffic. I board my return flight exhilarated and free, the way you feel when you've stepped cleanly out of something that no longer fits. I have no idea that the next long-distance phone call I take will belong to someone else entirely.

Back in Kuwait, I throw myself into work, though only briefly because my annual leave is approaching, and with it, a trip home for skiing and slow mornings before the summer's diplomatic whirlwind of stamping visas. I time my break for mid-March, before Easter; by June, the pace becomes relentless as everyone flees Kuwait's rising heat, thus needing visas to enter my home country.

By the time I head to my home country, the routine is familiar enough that they'll notice I'm gone. Marc and René are still only warm figures at my periphery, pleasant company, nothing more. I'm tired, guarded, not ready for anything new. Perhaps that's why Marc doesn't leave much of an impression at first. Still, the three of us fall into an easy habit of meeting at my place—backgammon on the blue sofa, something simple to eat, a few drinks before they head back to the desert.

Which is why I'm caught off guard when my phone buzzes. During my winter home leave, I retreat to the mountains, trading Kuwait's flat, endless sand for steep white slopes, powdery and untouched, the air sharp enough to sting my cheeks. At the lodge, I unclip my skis, slip my gloves into my pocket, and catch the vibration of my new cell phone. The display shows a number I know by heart—the UN headquarters line in Kuwait. The call is from Marc. He must be paying a small fortune for the connection; and yet, he dials.

The conversation lasts only minutes. The details blur— something about his observation post, maybe a question about the rotation schedule or when I'm due back. What stays with me is the sensation it leaves behind: a flicker of lightness, a faint current of excitement, and a quiet, uninvited delight.

Why it lands so sharply, I wish I knew. Maybe it's the fact that he thought to call at all. Maybe it's the sound of his voice —unhurried, warm—breaking into the gentle pace of my holiday. Or maybe it's that I didn't expect him to notice my absence, much less bridge it across continents.

Whatever the reason, something tilts. Maybe that's why I rush to change my ticket, shaving days off my leave to fly back early. Maybe that's why I choose the short, bold skirt for the ambassador's party, a choice meant, perhaps unconsciously, to stand out. To be seen.

I return to Kuwait sun-kissed, rested, and entirely unaware that someone is about to shift everything.

CHAPTER 3

The Night He Finally Sees Me

It's late March, just over a week since I came back from annual leave, and already Kuwait feels different. Or maybe it's me. I don't mean to shock anyone, but tonight, I do.

I arrive in the courtyard of the ambassador's residence to the low murmur of conversation and the clink of glassware. It's an obligatory cocktail party in honor of a minor dignitary from my home country. The desert air is warm, the sky tinted gold by the setting sun, which casts long shadows across the flagstone floor. Expatriates in business attire mingle with Kuwaiti guests in finely pressed *dishdashas*, their politeness edged with fatigue from days and nights that rarely end early. Some guests stifle yawns behind discreet hands as they raise their glasses in a half-hearted toast, crystal catching the ambient light. In Kuwait, alcohol is officially banned. But diplomats are allowed to import it for official functions, and so the rules bend here too—champagne flutes in the open air of a diplomatic terrace, the occasional bottle secretly poured behind closed doors. It's a gray area, like so much in Kuwait.

I'm in a navy-blue skirt that skims just above my knees, the fabric swaying as I cross the terrace. My fitted blazer, also navy, hugs my shoulders, while a crisp white sleeveless top peeks out beneath. A simple silver chain with a small pendant rests against my collarbone—I catch someone glancing at it as I shake hands—and matching silver studs glint softly at my ears. The golden tan on my skin speaks of solitary afternoons spent by the pool this past week, basking under the sun's warm embrace. It's not a look I usually plan, but tonight, it strikes the right chord.

I move through the space, noticing heads turning to follow my path. A colleague from the embassy passes by and grins. "You've brought the sparkle with you," he says, raising his glass slightly. I thank him lightly, momentarily caught off guard by the ease of his compliment. Others follow—strangers, polite and curious—and I find myself threading between small clusters of admiration that form around me.

Then my eyes land on Marc and René, unmistakable in their desert fatigues, standing casually by the bar. They're lazily picking at a mound of chilled Kuwaiti prawns, their fingers deftly navigating the icy platter, while their other hands cradle delicate wine glasses. The reception is loud enough that conversations blend into a soft buzz beneath the clink of glassware.

My skirt carries the weight of a small, private dare, not inappropriate, but shorter than usual. I tell myself it's just because of the heat, but when Marc's eyes, a flicker of blue, quick and bright, like lightning flashing behind clouds, find mine across the terrace, the thought I had before leaving home comes back to me in a rush.

To be seen.

Marc's face is a mixture of delight and disbelief, his usual stoicism breaking for a breath, leaving him suddenly vulnerable. His impossibly blue eyes, usually guarded, flicker with a spark that sends an unexpected thrill through me—a spark I realize I've been waiting for. He's always noticed me, but in that instant, I know he's letting me notice him back.

I make my way over, smiling as I gesture toward an empty table nearby. "Shall we sit?" I ask, already half-turning. They follow without hesitation, and a moment later we're seated around a small, round table on the edge of the bustling patio. A waiter approaches, balancing a tray with practiced ease, and hands me a refreshing bottle of beer, its exterior already shimmering with droplets of condensation. Marc and René signal for another round of their favorite red wine. Turning the cool bottle in my hands, I launch into stories about my home leave, describing the crisp air of the snowy mountains, the warmth of hearty family dinners filled with laughter, and the comforting familiarity of home. Yet, despite these pleasures, I confess how much I unexpectedly missed the vibrant life in Kuwait.

I raise my bottle as their glasses meet in a cheerful clink. A gentle breeze sweeps through the patio area, lifting strands of my hair, and in that moment, I am filled with clarity and renewal. I am back from home, unburdened from a relationship that no longer suited me, and ready to embrace whatever adventure awaits next.

That night marked something new—not because of Marc, not yet, but because I felt lighter. I had shed the last traces of the long-distance relationship that had gone nowhere. And suddenly I was free—available first and foremost to myself, and to whatever lay ahead.

Later that evening, the three of us return to my flat for a nightcap, our laughter echoing up the two flights of stairs as we climb. We settle into our usual spots around the worn wooden table. It's easy between us—too easy. René, with his mischievous grin, tosses out a string of jokes that have us chuckling, while I reach for the chilled beers, the bottles clinking softly as I hand them over. Marc methodically unfolds the backgammon board, his fingers deftly arranging the pieces with familiar precision. As I glance up to see his move, I notice it again—that very subtle flicker in his clear blue eyes, a fleeting spark that seems to dance beneath the surface. He's not openly flirting; instead, he's playing a game of his own, always two steps ahead, pretending otherwise. I let out a laugh, trying to brush it off, but inside, a strange sensation stirs, a feeling that seems out of place in this circle of friends. Our eyes meet briefly, a secretive glance exchanged, followed by a flicker of warmth. I remind myself, as if chanting a mantra, that Marc isn't meant for me. He knows it, too. And still, the unspoken tension lingers in the air.

Only much later—weeks later, when the truth no longer risks anything—does he confess: He brought René with him that night not for company. Not for fun. But because he knew. He knew that if we were alone, he wouldn't be able to keep his hands off me.

A few days later, they invite me to their flat for an evening of beer and backgammon, as has become our usual routine. However, this time, everything takes a different turn. We gather around the low, wooden table, the soft hum of the air conditioner filling the room, as René sits across from me, seemingly lost in thought, his gaze fixed intently on the backgammon board.

Marc is playing three games at once: one with René, one with me, and one with himself, trying not to break the rules he no longer believes in.

"Your move," he says, casual. Too casual. His voice is even, his eyes locked on mine, their blueness sharpened by something unspoken, even slightly dangerous—watching me, not the board.

I glance down. I have no idea what move I'm supposed to make.

Under the table, his foot finds mine. And doesn't move away. I don't flinch. I don't play coy. We both know what we're doing.

As he lights a cigarette, his finger grazes mine, and we both hold each other's gaze, neither willing to break the moment. In plain sight of René, Marc's fingers begin tracing slow, deliberate circles on my arm, sending a shiver through me. In that instant, the moment unfolds like something always meant to be, an inevitability we had both sensed from the start.

I act as if nothing is unfolding around us, so when René finally retreats to his room—whether driven by the palpable tension or sheer exhaustion—I barely register his exit. We are left in a profound silence, each of us bracing for whatever might follow.

As the first light of dawn begins to creep into the room, I rise abruptly, seize my bag, and mutter that it's time for me to leave. Marc, ever the gentleman, immediately stands as well and escorts me to my car with a sense of urgency matching mine, the air thick with unspoken words.

Outside, it's already warm, a warmth that clings as I step to the curb and reach for the driver's door. I turn, braced for a gentle farewell, but he crosses the distance in a heartbeat and kisses me—fierce, certain, the culmination of every footsie touch and lingering glance. For a beat I'm startled, caught off guard by the certainty of it, but then I yield. His lips are warm, insistent, tasting of wine and salt, his tongue coaxing mine into a slow, urgent dance. My fingers knot into his shirt as his hands gingerly find my waist, and a heavy sigh escapes me, surrendering to the rush of heat that surges through. Time stretches; the world falls away.

And then his eyes. That impossible, electric blue that has undone me from the start. Open, unguarded, locked on mine as his mouth deepens the kiss. He doesn't see the tan, the skirt, the surface I offer. He sees the raw center of me: the girl I was, the woman I haven't yet met. His gaze strips away every pretense, and for the first time I feel completely, terrifyingly seen.

When we finally pull apart, I don't speak. There's nothing to add. His kiss has said it all—desire, surrender, inevitability. I slide into the car, hands trembling slightly on the steering wheel, and pull away. Not in triumph, but in wonder. Not of conquest, but of being chosen, seen, remembered. The early morning air feels altered, charged with what has just begun. Something has shifted, and neither of us pretends otherwise.

CHAPTER 4

The Call from the Desert

The day after our first kiss, I prepare myself for the usual, heavy silence that often follows such moments. In those pre-smartphone days, you waited anxiously for a reassuring call to confirm that the kiss wasn't a figment of your imagination. Sometimes, that anticipation was met with disappointment. But not this time.

The phone rings at the perfect moment, just as I've pushed away the remains of my lunchtime sandwich. His voice crackles through the land line from the arid expanse of the desert, from the distant DMZ, from his observation point

I sink into my worn blue sofa, its fabric soft against my skin, and light a cigarette, feeling the tension within me unravel at the sound of his voice. It's warm and familiar, imbued with a confident ease, and I can almost see the smile stretching across his face. We chat about the mundane details of our days—the rising heat, the repetitive routines—our words skimming the surface of more profound thoughts, never quite touching upon the kiss itself.

The conversation is brief, yet it carries a significance that lingers. I lean back against the cushions, watching the cigarette smolder to a stub in the ashtray, the receiver still warm against my palm. I can't help but wonder what comes next. The weight of the line we've crossed hangs between us—an unspoken understanding that neither of us desires, or even can, retreat from.

Later, as I mentally sift through each moment—the ambassador's party, the murmur of voices and warm light stretching into the night, the unexpected kiss that tasted of beer and wine, and the quiet fraying that spread like a delicate thread—I realize our story didn't begin with that electrifying meeting of lips. It began on the snow-dusted slopes, when the sharp ring of my phone cut through the crisp mountain air. It began with my decision to leave the comfort of home and my family and head back early. It was in the silent certainty that filled my chest, a certainty that I was no longer merely coasting through life. I was deliberately leaning in, stepping toward something new.

We never make any concrete plans, no plans for evenings by the pool or in hotel lounges, no whispered promises of evenings spent wrapped in each other's arms, no specific dates marked on the calendar. Honestly, I have no idea where that impulsive kiss will take us, if anywhere at all. There's a persistent part of me that never forgets he's married. That reality lingers like a shadow, even during moments when he seems to let it slip from his mind.

As his work schedule at the UN observation post in the desert is unpredictable and far away from Kuwait City, I carry on with my own life, immersing myself in my demanding job, catching up with friends at the mall, and maintaining my own schedule. Still, we speak every day once I clock out from work, sometimes even more often. What do we talk about? Everything and nothing all at once. He tells me about his childhood in a small industrial town, the day he first met his wife at a bustling city café, and her successful career as a lawyer—details he shares with a mixture of pride and nostalgia. There's no hint of secrecy in his voice, just the candidness of a man recounting the story of his life. I listen, not because I feel guilty, but with a cautious interest, holding tightly to the boundaries I insist still stand firm.

I reciprocate by sharing snippets of my own story: the constant relocations as a diplomat's child, the overwhelming loneliness, and the perpetual need to adapt to new cultures and languages. What I don't say—not yet—is how those moves, each one an inescapable uprooting, left hairline cracks in me that I learned to ignore. How the endless starting over taught me resilience, but also a restlessness I can't always brush away. At the time, I think of it only as a quirk of my upbringing. Later, I'll understand it was something more. For now, I simply notice how Marc's calming voice on the other end of the line comes as an anchor I didn't know I'd been searching for.

At the time, I still think this is a friendship. Hoping against hope that the kiss was a one-time thing—a moment of heat, a release of pressure, nothing more. I believe, truly, that men and women can be friends. That's what I tell myself in this case as well. And maybe, in another place, under different skies, that would have been true.

Each call we share fuels a slow-burning longing like steam steadily building pressure in a sealed pot. The intensity of my emotions is overwhelming, and I sit on my blue sofa, surrounded by the haze of cigarette smoke, torn by the thoughts swirling in my mind. We both envision the night when we'll lie entwined, our limbs a comforting mess, and we joke, almost every time, about having a leisurely bath together, the kind of throwaway fantasy that somehow becomes a standing invitation between us, but doubt is mine alone. I question whether this connection can, or should, be more than friendship. A gentle, persistent tug at my heart whispers insistently, but uncertainty lingers, leaving me caught between longing and restraint.

He still can't commit to a specific date for his return to the city. "Maybe next week, maybe not," he teases with a nonchalance that only heightens my anticipation. So I wait, tracing invisible calendars in my mind, even though no date is circled. While I've dated military men before, there's a profound difference this time: the calls continue to flow, and so does the craving that lingers long after the receiver has been placed back on its cradle.

It's Friday evening, April 10th—a date that will eventually hold significant importance, though I'm unaware of it now. I'm dressed in my favorite navy blouse and white linen slacks, ready to drive to my German friends' barbecue, the smell of fresh perfume lingering in the air, when my new Kuwaiti cell phone buzzes loudly on the bedroom counter. It's him. His buoyant voice crackles through the line, "I'm coming into the city—just for tonight. I know I shouldn't, but I can't help myself. I need to see you. To feel you."

My heart thuds like a drum, each beat echoing with his youthful, boyish excitement that borders on recklessness. I can hardly catch my breath.

At the barbecue, I weave through clusters of chattering guests, the aroma of grilled sausages and infectious laughter filling the air, but nothing seems real. I hold my expression just a touch too bright, concealing the joyful anticipation beneath the surface, and glance at my watch every couple of minutes, counting down until I can discreetly slip away.

The highway is a sea of brake lights, cars crawling along in the Friday-night traffic that Kuwait is infamous for, reminiscent of a busy Sunday in the West. I'm on my way home, gripping the steering wheel tightly, a bead of sweat trickling down my temple as I anxiously watch the clock, fearing I'll arrive too late. I make it, pulling up to my place barely in time. At 10:30 p.m., the ding-dong of the doorbell signals his arrival.

He steps inside my apartment without hesitation, the desert air still clinging to him, carrying with it the faint scent of dust and diesel. My gaze drops to his left hand, and I realize: the gold band is gone. Not forgotten, not lost, but left behind on purpose. The skin beneath it is pale, untouched by the sun, a visible imprint of the life that waits elsewhere. For a beat, I wonder if he knows I'll notice. Of course he does.

Our eyes meet, and words become unnecessary—the unspoken charge of two people who have spent countless calls teasing about this moment. His desert boots are deftly unlaced and discarded by the door when my hand finds his, and we move toward the bathroom with the burning certainty of a plan long in the making. The steam from the waiting bath curls into the hallway, warm and scented, wrapping around us like a promise.

Finally, I'm unguarded—not exposed, but seen. And suddenly, I want to see him, too. Not just the man I talk to every day. Not the uniform. Him. More of him.

So I begin.

I undo each button slowly, carefully—not to tease, not to test. But because it matters. Like I'm peeling away something that doesn't belong between us anymore. His shirt, his undershirt, the belt still warm from his body. The desert dust clings faintly to the fabric. I don't brush it off. I let it fall.

He stands there, still and quiet, not watching me with hunger but with a kind of reverence, as though this moment is rare even for him. And I haven't had it either. Not like this.

There's no rush. Just the slow trace of my hands, the sound of our breathing. It feels... celebratory. Not in the loud way. In the way a prayer can be a celebration. In the way truth is. When I finally look up, his mouth curves in delight, as if to say: Thank you. I'm yours, too.

I light candles, their glow flickering across the tiles, and let soft music spill into the room. He steps closer, his fingers finding the first button of my blouse. One by one, they slip free. The brush of his knuckles makes me shiver.

"You've done this before," I murmur, a smile tugging at my lips. His answering look holds both mischief and certainty.

My blouse falls, then the rest, each piece leaving me lighter, more exposed, until only his gaze remains on me. His mouth grazes my neck, slow and deliberate, and I have to close my eyes to steady myself. I need the pause, a breath between the shiver and what comes next, so I turn to the tub and test the water—it glistens invitingly.

I ease myself into the tub. He slips in behind me, his body pressing close, unmistakable in its wanting, the water rippling with our every shift. His hands begin a tender journey across my skin, not rushed, not demanding—savoring, sharing. We sip wine, trade soft laughter, and let the candlelight blur the edges of the moment. I lean back into him, eyes closed, and release the last of my tension—shoulders, jaw, heart.

We stay there for a long while, long enough for the water to cool, for the candles to burn lower, for our fingers to prune and our conversation to fall into comfortable silences. Only then do we rise, reluctant but smiling, a warmth passing between us without words.

He dries me slowly, memorizing my form with each deliberate stroke. I return the favor. It's still all reverent, not frantic.

We don't hasten to the bedroom; we're already in an intimate embrace. When we finally glide beneath the sheets, it's a fluid transition—our bodies instinctively know the way. The bedroom is dimly lit, candles casting a gentle flicker. The cool sheets welcome me as I recline; he follows, not with urgency, but with a tender arrival, softly, entirely. His lips find mine once more, slower, gentler, as though discovering me anew. His hands explore, not to conquer, but out of sheer curiosity. I shiver when he pauses to truly look at me, seeing something unique in his eyes: not just desire, but genuine care. We attune to each other's breath, chuckle at the occasional awkwardness, and tenderly cradle each other's faces. When we finally unite, it's not the peak that overwhelms me, but everything leading up to and following it.

Later, as we lay entwined beneath the cooling sheet, the rhythmic hum of the air conditioner filling the room, he gently presses his lips to my shoulder. We don't speak—we don't need to. But we know something has begun. A boundary has been crossed, subtly but unmistakably. This is no longer flirtation or possibility. It's real now. And I'm beginning to understand what that means.

Sleep eludes us as we try to reclaim what distance kept from us, our shared silence speaking volumes. In the stillness of the night, we make love again, each movement deliberate, each touch a reminder. It is not about discovery but about cherishing and holding tight to what we know will eventually slip away.

As the first light of dawn creeps through the curtains, he dresses in his uniform with a composed grace, his movements gentle and precise. He presses a tender kiss to my shoulder once more before he silently retreats back to the vast emptiness of the desert. He has been with me for seven hours

—not the longest I've ever spent with a man, but different in a way I can't quite name. It isn't the length of the hours. It's the way they felt: complete, unhurried, like nothing was borrowed.

The First Time I Felt Fully Wanted

I had known other men. Kind men. Charming men. Men who had wanted parts of me—my body, my stories, my silence. But Marc had been different. He hadn't taken; he had received. And in doing so, he had given something back. It hadn't just been the sex. It had been what came after. The way he had looked at me—clear, unashamed. The way he hadn't corrected me. The way he had let me be soft, and never made me feel wrong for it. That had been the first time I felt fully wanted. Not in pieces. Not conditionally. Not with caution. All of me. And I believed—no, I knew—that it had changed something in me forever.

After he has left, I lay there, the room silent save for my own heartbeat pounding with vibrant intensity. Long-buried emotions surge within me, flooding me with a newfound awareness, a life I had never dared to claim.

I never asked. Not him. Not myself. I didn't wonder what went on in his mind—whether he thought about his wife, whether he told himself she was far away and would never find out. She didn't, apparently. Did he not care? Was it calculated? Or was it just... human? I didn't know. And at the time, I didn't want to know. Only now—all these years later—did I find myself asking. Not because I regretted it. I didn't. But because I saw things differently now. With more softness. And more clarity. There was so much I had chosen not to see.

I go to work on Saturday, the start of the workweek. That's my way. I sort visa applications. I stamp passports. I answer the same travel questions I've been asked a hundred times before. But I'm not really there. My body, alive despite the fatigue, moves through the motions, but my mind is somewhere else entirely—still steeped in candlelight and bathwater, still tracing the memory of his hands, his breath, the way he saw me when I undressed him like it meant something. The fluorescent lights in my office feel too bright. Every voice too sharp. Even my tea tastes wrong. And underneath it all, I carry something soft and unfamiliar—not regret, not guilt. Just… fullness. Like I've stepped into a new version of myself, and the old one hasn't quite caught up yet.

Two weeks drift by, each day blending into the next. My job keeps me busy, buried under stacks of paperwork and passports, while he's stationed at a tense post-war border, his eyes always scanning the horizon. These days stretch endlessly yet slip through my fingers like sand. We've fallen into a comforting routine: every afternoon, after the grind of work and the quiet of lunch, I sink into the cushions of the worn blue sofa, a cigarette perched between my fingers, and we talk for forty-five minutes. It's the brightest part of my otherwise monotonous days. We revisit that magical first night, recalling every glance exchanged, every kiss that left us breathless, every whispered word. To my surprise, reliving those moments together carries almost the same thrill as when they happened.

On a few occasions, he manages to make it into Kuwait City, slipping away from his post overnight. We don't go out. We don't need to. We spend the time tucked away in my apartment, wrapped in each other, making love, sharing simple meals, and letting the world outside fall away.

Later, I pour my heart into my diary: I'm loving my life. And my life with Marc. He's more attentive, more present, kinder than anyone I've ever known, the whole of him wrapping around me like a warm embrace. I never imagined such depth of connection was possible. Yet, I set a rule for myself: don't fall in love.

As hard as I tried—and I did—I couldn't keep it, of course. I fell hard, quickly, totally, yet I knew that if I did fall, that's where the real pain would begin. That's where wanting more would become unbearable. And I also knew this wouldn't last.

I think, just for a moment, about asking if there could be more, something lasting, something beyond this hidden space we've carved out for ourselves. The question hovers on the edge of my breath, but I don't say it. And he doesn't ask either.

We both know the answer. Not because we've spoken it, but because it's already there—in the way we hold each other, and in the way we let go. This isn't a love that gets to stay. We never name it, never make promises we can't keep. But that harsh truth hangs in the background, shaping everything. And maybe that's why every moment cuts sharper than it should. Sweeter. Sadder. Lit with a kind of urgency I can't shake, as if we're always just a breath away from goodbye.

Our connection runs so deep, I feel it in my very bones: had we crossed paths two years earlier, we would have married without hesitation. Those two years, that chasm of time, cost us everything. We talk about the wretched timing more than we should, knowing there's nothing we can do to change it, and dwelling on it would unravel the fragile joy we've found.

A Foreign Country

I once asked him how he justified living this split life. He said, lightly, "It's a deliberate act of charity in a foreign land." I heard the weight in his words. He needed to make it noble—to give himself to two women, one by promise and one by presence. He cared too much to call it what it was. Years later, I admit that phrase wounded me, not because it was cruel, but because it wasn't. He believed it. He relied on it. And in a strange way, so did I.

He says it lightly, matter-of-factly, and I know he doesn't mean it as condescension. What he's really saying is that we're both lonely here, and this—whatever we've stepped into—keeps that loneliness from swallowing us whole. It's a kindness we give each other, not a favor one of us bestows.

So I focus on the present: our evenings, our calls, our laughter, the way he looks at me like I'm all he sees. I tell myself to live fully, since there's no tidy ending, no clear path forward. But I also refuse to live with regrets—not for this, not for him.

CHAPTER 5

The Island

It's the first week of May before Marc is able to return to the city for more than a handful of hours—and by luck, it's my weekend. The moment he tells me, I call Ania and Badr, my constant companions on so many Thursdays past, to ask if they're headed to Umm al Maradem. We all know it simply as *The Island*, a slender, uninhabited strip of sand adrift in the pale blue off Kuwait's coast.

The Island is untouched by the clutter of civilization: no buildings to cast shadows, no services to intrude upon the solitude, and no inquisitive minds to disturb the peace. This was the first fragment of Kuwaiti soil liberated from Iraqi occupation, and for a cherished ten hours, it offers a rare refuge from Kuwait's stringent no-alcohol regulations, if only because no one is there to enforce them.

I've been there more times than I can count, always with Ania and Badr. Sometimes I brought boyfriends along, other times it was just the three of us, the day unfolding in an easy drift of salt air and companionship. But this time will be different. This time, Marc is coming along—and somehow, that changes everything. The familiar takes on a newness, as if the island itself might be watching us.

I always enjoy the drive south to the bustling marina where Badr moor his boat, not just for the destination, but for the refinery corridor along the way. The highway traces a straight line toward Saudi Arabia, bordered by colossal oil complexes that rise majestically like steel cathedrals against the horizon. By nightfall, these structures become utterly captivating—flare stacks ignite, burning off excess gas in a fiery dance, while a constellation of lights illuminates the path, guiding travelers through the inky expanse of desert to the left. Even for a weekend morning, the traffic is dense, not only because this is the solitary route to Saudi Arabia, but also due to the Kuwaiti passion for their yachts, some of which are so grand they could easily be mistaken for small ships.

Badr's boat, a sleek, white vessel with a polished deck and a sturdy hull, is both simple and dependable. It boasts a powerful engine capable of slicing through turbulent seas and seats for eight passengers, ensuring comfort and camaraderie.

Marc and I arrive at the dock, arms laden with coolers brimming with chilled water bottles, frosty cans of beer, and trays of marinated chicken, exuding a tantalizing aroma of garlic and herbs. The sun blazes high in the cobalt sky, casting sharp shadows, and though a tawny sandstorm brews on the distant horizon, our friends assure us it will steer clear of the island. They even promise a sunset that will paint the sky with breathtaking colors.

Laughing with excitement, we clamber aboard, exchanging hugs and cheerful greetings. We carefully stow away our umbrellas, intricately designed shishas, and ice chests filled with refreshments. The sea lies before us, a vast expanse of glassy, tranquil blue. The engine roars to life, a deep, throaty growl, and the bow rises as we surge forward at full throttle.

I settle into a seat at the stern, feeling the vibration of the engine beneath me. Marc wraps his arm around me, his fingers lightly tracing patterns along my neck and shoulder, sending a pleasant shiver down my spine. My hand rests comfortably on his thigh, nestled against the fabric of his navy shorts.

Ania glances back at me from her position near the helm. Her eyes meet mine, and I break into a wide grin, unable to hide the joy bubbling within me. She nods in approval, her own expression a mirror of my happiness, as the boat cuts through the water, leaving a sparkling wake behind us.

I'm grateful that both Ania and Badr immediately warm to Marc, their genuine cordiality and open arms signaling his seamless entry into our cherished weekend ritual. No one pries about our relationship status, which is obvious anyway; when I casually introduce him, acceptance passes between them, and the matter rests there. In our tight-knit circle, judgment is a foreign concept. Our motto is simple: it is what it is — a philosophy that suits us perfectly.

After forty-five minutes of cruising across the expansive Gulf, we begin to decelerate as the island emerges, shimmering like a mirage in the distance. The water near the shallows is so clear that I can see the intricate patterns of sunlight dancing on the sandy bottom, while schools of fish dart playfully in our wake. I slip on my water shoes, the snug fit wrapping my feet, and wait for the familiar signal. Marc, with his usual enthusiasm, is right behind me, ready to leap as soon as we're close enough. Badr, a seasoned sailor, skillfully guides the boat, cutting the engine with a practiced hand, and we drift gently toward the inviting sandy shore. He steps carefully into the water, moving with deliberate caution to avoid the starfish and spiny sea urchins, before letting the anchor drop with a soft splash. The line pulls taut, the boat settles into place, and in the next instant Marc and I plunge overboard, the warm Gulf water rising around us as the island waits ahead. He surfaces laughing, shaking the droplets from his hair. "Like a bath — but better," he grins. I splash him lightly, grinning back. "Careful, or I'll make you prove that tonight."

Still laughing, we wade ashore and start unloading our gear and begin to set up camp: large towels spread across the warm sand, oversized pillows piled under the shade of wide umbrellas, the portable grill positioned carefully to catch the breeze. Ania assembles her shisha pipe while Badr props up the small folding table for backgammon. It's casual but deliberate, a shared ritual, practiced and familiar.

Soon we're sprawled in the shade, sinking into the softness of the pillows as the grill crackles nearby, sending the scent of roasting meat into the salty air. Fragrant shisha smoke drifts lazily on the breeze while we play backgammon, the clatter of dice punctuating our laughter. Ania sits cross-legged, eyes fixed on the board, while Marc stretches out beside her, his back resting against my knees as if it's the most natural thing in the world. I pretend to read a paperback, but my gaze keeps drifting—to the ease between us, the sun-bleached drift of the late morning, the way his hand absently brushes sand from my leg, like we've always been here.

Every so often, we slip away to the boat—just the two of us, the sea softly swaying beneath us. Out there, everything strips back to simplicity. We move between talk and touch, sometimes slow and hushed, sometimes not. It's not about performance. It's about the privacy, the permission to just be in each other's orbit, without interruption.

Later, as we return to shore, the afternoon stretches out— sun-warmed skin, damp towels, shared glances that say more than words. The world stays at a distance, held back by the gentle rolling of the waves and the easy rhythm we've fallen into, just for now.

The entire day unfolds without the weight of Kuwait's stringent regulations hanging over us. We laugh openly, sip drinks without looking over our shoulders, and hold each other close with an unapologetic ease. The island presents itself in its purest form: the warmth of the sun kissing our skin, the saltwater splashing playfully against our legs, and the comforting presence of friends who are like family.

All too soon, the sun begins to dip, casting long shadows across the sand. It's time to pack up. We move quickly, the way we always do—towels shaken out, dishes rinsed in seawater, everything tucked back into bags as if we were never here.

On the way back, the boat's powerful engines roar, vibrating through the hull as we cut across the evening water. The sea is calmer now, streaked with light. We sit as we did on the way to the island, side by side in the back of the boat, the wind tugging at my sun-streaked hair, our faces still glowing from a day in the sun. The sky shifts from gold to rose to something deeper, and Marc traces idle circles on my arm—a private game that feels more daring than the sea around us. The shoreline grows closer, and with it, the almost sobering return to reality.

A few seabirds trail behind us, wings skimming the surface like they're not quite ready to go home either.

Back on the mainland, we exchange warm hugs with our hosts, their faces carrying the easy promise of future visits. We assure them we'll be back soon, our words filled with sincerity. In the car, Marc's fingers lace through mine, a familiar and comforting grip, as we replay every cherished moment, already casting it in the amber glow of nostalgia. I glance through the window and see the towering oil refineries lighting up the night sky like a sprawling second city, their fiery glow a constant reminder that the everyday world still waits for us beyond this island escape.

Outside of our weekend retreats to the island, life is narrower. More contained. We slip back into our routines—my embassy work, his long drives, our errands in the heat and evenings behind closed doors. But somehow, Marc makes even the smallest moments vibrate with charge. He shows up with pulsating energy, like he's fully present even when we're just making coffee or folding laundry.

He's not dramatic in his lovemaking. Nothing is rushed. Everything between us unfolds slowly, through small conversations and silent exchanges, the kind that says more than words ever could. A glance across the room. A raised eyebrow. A low "This okay?" before his fingers brush against mine.

It's a give-and-take we fall into without a word A kind of choreography we invent as we go. We check in often, not because we doubt, but because we care. Every decision—to stay a little longer, to touch, to trust—is made together.

Given the circumstances, nothing about this—our—life is easy. But it's real. And for now, that's enough.

I feel wanted, undoubtedly. But deeper than that, I feel enveloped in a sense of safety. I feel truly seen and understood. In him, I have found a place to call home. For the first time in ages, contentment floods me—I am truly happy. The uncertainty of what lies ahead can wait in the wings. I remind myself, as many times as necessary, "We'll cross that bridge when we get to it."

For now, we have *The Island*. We have each other. And we have a bed that wraps us in warmth, a place we find almost impossible to leave.

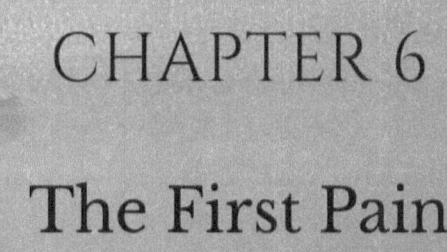

CHAPTER 6

The First Pain

It's early May, just about a month since we first crossed that line. One night over grilled fish and a bottle of cold white wine, he says it like he's talking about the weather. "End of May. Cyprus. Ten days." His wife will fly in, and he will meet her there. The visit has been on the books for months, penciled into a life I'm not part of. He says it lightly, almost kindly, as if softening the edge. I lift my glass, pretending the words don't catch. But they do. They always will.

The real ache is mine. It begins just before he heads off to Cyprus, sharp and certain, like something I've been bracing for without knowing it. I'm counting down the days with dread. He, I suspect, is counting them down with mounting anticipation. His legal wife isn't a distant idea—she's in Europe right now, flesh and blood, waiting for him. United Nations tours don't include family. No spouses. No children. Just uniforms, the desert, and an endless cycle of relief teams —soldiers rotating in and out, replacing one another.

My assignment carries a different weight, rooted in routine, tethered to embassy protocol and a residence permit that gives the illusion of permanence. His world is all transience: checkpoints, dust, and long silences interrupted by brief bursts of life.

And yet, right now, in this in-between, I'm the one he comes home to. Not officially. Not forever. But in every way that counts, in the hours we steal, in the way he lets the door close behind him and drops his keys into the dish like it means something.

This is the first conjugal visit since we started seeing each other—we both knew it was coming, but foreknowledge sharpens the pain. It's not just his absence that unravels me, but the certainty that he will sleep beside someone else—his wife—whisper the words he's whispered to me, before returning, however briefly, to the life we've built in stolen moments. A vicious jealousy rises in me, one I scarcely admit even to myself. I remind myself: we agreed to this. I chose it. Yet my heart never signed on.

The week leading up to his departure, we act as if nothing is amiss: dinners with friends, shared jokes, public laughter. He rarely looks at anyone else, and while part of me cherishes this connection, another part wonders if I'm losing myself in it.

About two weeks before he leaves, the expat summer ball at the International Hotel arrives and marks the high point of the spring season, and our chance to pretend nothing is ending. I slip into a flowing white dress adorned with delicate pale blue polka dots, the fabric cool against my skin. Marc is dressed tailored gray trousers that complement his crisp white shirt, a navy bow tie perfectly knotted at his throat, and a matching jacket that sits effortlessly on his shoulders. When we pause in front of the floor-length mirror on our way out the door, I gasp. We could have stepped out of a postcard. Or a promise. His hand finds the small of my back. Our reflections lean into each other without effort. We fit. Undeniably.

"Look at us," he murmurs. I let out a breath of laughter, stunned.

This is how it's meant to be.

And for one dangerous second, I let myself believe it could be.

Walking into the ball hand in hand, we step as though into another life. Outside by the pool, round tables of eight or ten are already filling with expatriates from Italy, France, America, and Germany. Illicit beer and wine flow freely—the wine decanted into glass carafes, the beer tucked into frosted glasses, both hiding in plain sight. The air is soft and weighted, thick with warmth and the distant sound of laughter. The blue water of the pool shimmers in the floodlights. Golden lights strung between palm trees, the faint clink of glassware, and the murmur of expats trying not to talk about work. René is there, impeccably dressed, sharing a joke with our German friends near the drinks table. We join them, all easy conversation and second rounds.

There is even a live music band, and when the music drifts across the water, for a few hours, everything drifts into suspension: heat, history, even caution. Marc doesn't ask so much as offer—his hand extended, his posture straight.

"May I?" he says, his voice even.

But something in his eyes is already dancing. We twirl and sway, our feet barely brushing the polished tiles. Laughter ripples through the night, and bubbles of joy dance in our veins as we nearly stumble into the pool, breathless and unsteady with everything unspoken between us.

No one comments on our closeness. No one questions the stolen glances or the way his hand rests at my waist a little longer than necessary. I'm a little surprised, honestly. I expected someone—anyone—to raise an eyebrow, to make a joke, to pull me aside. But no one does.

Maybe they choose to see only what fits the narrative of polite blindness. Or maybe they silently accept that this is part of the price we all pay for living away from home, a loosening of rules, a quiet agreement not to look too closely at the lives we build far from consequence.

In those fleeting hours before dawn, it's as if the world grants us a temporary reprieve, a moment of absolution under the fading stars. But as the sky begins to lighten, the unavoidable truth edges closer: I know he will return to her. And the weight of that inevitable goodbye settles over me like the low, ominous rumble of a distant storm.

In the days leading up to his departure, we establish a comforting routine amid the simmering chaos of us, of everything we have become and everything we know we can never be. Our meals are uncomplicated yet satisfying, prepared with the limited ingredients we manage to find, as we savor each bite at a small, worn-out table in my kitchen. We exchange books, their pages slightly frayed and yellowed, absorbing ourselves in stories that provide a temporary escape from reality. The television murmurs gently in the background, offering snippets of normalcy as we engage in backgammon, the soft clatter of dice and the movement of pieces adding a sense of rhythm to our evenings. He sleeps by my side, our breathing synchronized, as though this has been our life for an eternity, despite the uncertainties looming ahead.

On certain afternoons, we venture to the deserted pool at his colleagues' empty apartment, an address he still helps pay for, just to sustain an illusion. The water, cool and clear, jolts us back to life, a stark contrast to the oppressive heat that clings to everything outside. We swim so closely, entwined in each other's presence, that it is as though we might merge into one being, drowning in our shared moments.

When impatience overcomes the fragile peace, we retreat indoors, slipping silently behind closed doors that guard our private world. In his temporary apartment—bare, functional, nothing personal—we find solace in each other's embrace. The air around us vibrates with the intensity of our connection, the walls absorbing the hum of our intertwined bodies, creating a sanctuary amid the madness of our own world.

As the weight of my days begins to build, I find myself craving a familiar voice. Gabby, a close friend from back home, agrees to visit—her second trip to Kuwait. I wait for her at the airport, rehearsing the moment in my head. What I'll say. How I'll say it. The exact moment I'll let the words fall: *I've found someone.*

And though I trust her, truly, a small part of me worries. Will she understand? Will she hold me in a different light— not with disapproval, but with unspoken confusion, or worse, pity? I hate that the thought even occurs to me. But it does.

Still, I know I'll tell her. Some truths insist on being spoken, even before we know how they'll be received.

When Gabby finally emerges into the arrivals hall, I notice her before she sees me. She looks travel-weary but familiar. The moment she spots me, her whole face lights up, crinkling at the corners with the same grin I've known for years. A giddy warmth rises in my chest before I can stop it. I haven't said a word yet, but I already know what I'm going to tell her. "I've found someone," the words stumble out of me before I can stop them. She doesn't blink. Just grins wider and pulls me into a hug. "I knew it," she urges. "Tell me everything."

On our way back from the airport to the embassy building, I share every detail: how I first saw him at the ambassador's cocktail party, the way he stood across the terrace with a glass of wine in his hand, how we played backgammon late into the night, and how he finally kissed me in the stillness just before dawn. And of course, I tell her about Marc's colleague René, with his gentle manners and an easy humor that puts everyone at ease. He strikes me as a perfect match for Gabby. She sits beside me, her head bobbing occasionally, her eyes dancing with curiosity as she hangs onto my every word.

As Gabby has been to Kuwait before, she settles in easily, driving around Kuwait City in my car, even as I go to work in the mornings. We spend the afternoons together exploring the many new malls that have opened since her last visit, and we visit my German friends for dinner. When Marc and René are in the city on their days off, we quickly form a tight-knit foursome—Marc, René, Gabby, and I—sharing lunches I've prepared with Gabby's help and evenings filled with laughter and conversation. It's the kind of camaraderie that only deepens as Marc's departure to Cyprus looms.

One languid afternoon, we hop into my dusty blue sedan and head south to a town called Ahmadi. There, the once-charred landscape of Kuwait's oilfields, scorched by the Iraqi army, is slowly being coaxed back to life, patches of green emerging from the blackened earth. René grips the steering wheel with a relaxed confidence, while Gabby chats animatedly in the passenger seat, her laughter punctuating the hum of the engine. Marc and I sit close in the back seat, our shoulders brushing. He leans in, his breath warm against my ear as he softly whispers in German, *"Ich hab dich sehr, sehr lieb."*

Not "I love you." Not Ich liebe dich. *Not the big declaration.*

Something gentler. Deeper. In German, Ich hab dich lieb *lives in the space between affection and devotion. Less theatrical than love. More intimate. It means: You matter to me. You belong with me. I feel safe with you.*

Even now, I can feel the breath of it on my skin. And I shiver.

As we tour the site under the relentless sun, clutching water bottles to stay hydrated in the brutal heat, our gazes catch in playful, stolen moments, a silent flirtation. Behind us, Gabby and René stroll leisurely, absorbed in their own world.

After we've had our fill of sun and heat, we're flushed and dusty, our clothes clinging to us. Back in Kuwait City, the four of us spill into my apartment, the air-conditioning hitting like a wave, peeling the afternoon from our skin. We linger in the cool, laughing as we trade the day's dust and sweat for fresh clothes and a hint of perfume, the easy chatter drifting from room to room. Someone opens a bottle of white wine, and we share a quick drink—just enough to loosen the edges—before heading out.

By early evening we're on our way to a Kuwaiti friend's wedding party, which at first carries the tedious air of formality, dull and restrained. The reception is strictly non-alcoholic, the air heavy with the murmur of polite conversation and the clinking of glasses filled only with fruit juice and sweet tea. Only when the vibrant music begins does the atmosphere transform. The rhythmic beats and lively tunes beckon us to the dance floor, where we start to move, drink, and laugh with carefree abandon.

By night's end, a noticeable connection has formed between René and Gabby, their laughter and lingering glances full of unspoken promises. Marc and I share a quick, knowing grin before deciding it's time for everyone to head back to my place. René agrees without hesitation, and we drive off through the night, the warm wind rushing past us, dry and heavy, the only kind Kuwait ever offers after sunset. Even an unexpected police checkpoint on the way doesn't dampen our spirits, merely slowing us for a brief moment.

Once home, Marc and I lead them to my bedroom, offering the comfort of the space, while we settle onto the pullout sofa in the living room. Marc playfully falls into an exaggerated sleep, snoring theatrically, a performance crafted just for René, who still seems blissfully unaware of our tender intimacy, shared just a few minutes later in the hushed shadows of the night.

The days that follow blur in color and heat. Parties, dinners, pool time. To give the men some space, Gabby and I visit the fabric souk, the one we both love. We haggle, sip tea, get measured for dresses we don't need, and run our hands over bolts of silk and cotton in colors so vivid they're a feast for the eyes.

One morning, with René back at his post, Marc, Gabby, and I join a guided embassy tour of Kuwait's state mosque, the largest in the country. It's the only time in my life I wear a head scarf, the fabric an unwelcome weight against my hair. I catch my reflection in the polished marble as we walk and it's as if I'm looking at someone else. Marc, walking just behind me, leans in and murmurs, "Not your style," amusement threading his voice. He knows. I offer him a fleeting grin that falters before it settles. Inside the mosque, the prayer hall stretches vast and open, the kind of space that makes you lower your voice without thinking. I still find myself oohing and ahhing at the marble floors and intricate calligraphy, though the space itself remains spare, almost austere.

Afterward, the three of us stop by the fish souk, where we marvel at what Kuwait's fisheries produce—baskets of tiny silver fish, as if spilled from a net of light; rows of fresh *hammour* laid out on ice; and the gleaming scales of *zobaidy* and *safi*.

And a few days later—*The Island*. This time, just Gabby, René, and me, invited by Ania and Badr. Marc, who's already returned to his post and therefore can't be with us, was the one who suggested the arrangement. While I love the time on the island with my friends, I miss him, my heart aching in a way I've already come to expect on the days he isn't around me, especially watching René and Gabby so effortlessly connected.

Much too soon, Gabby packs her suitcase. As we drive to the airport in the heavy heat of the afternoon, we talk about how much fun we've had these past two weeks with all the dinners, the dancing, the heat, the absurd little adventures. Who would have thought that a country like Kuwait—so strict, so restrained—could offer so much laughter? She hugs me hard before she goes, promising to write, to call, to come back soon. I stand there for a while after she disappears into the terminal, watching the crowds swallow her.

I'm glad she came. Glad she had her little adventure with René, a flirtation that never grew into more. Part of me is relieved she didn't fall as hard as I have. It would have been too much to witness someone else tumbling into the same impossible longing.

And when Gabby leaves, René disappears too. Not for any reason we speak aloud, only because Marc and I pull the world in tighter, keeping what's left for ourselves.

As I drive home alone from the airport, I'm struck by the emptiness she leaves behind, the echo of laughter in my apartment, the easy distraction of having her here. Her visit made everything feel lighter, if only for a while. Now, with her gone, I'm left with too much space. Too much quiet. And the knowledge that the next days will be the hardest yet.

The night before he leaves for Cyprus, we sit together on my blue sofa. He wears shorts and an undershirt. I curl into him, legs tucked under, familiar now. Outside, the last days of May press against the windows, the heat thick and unmoving, even as the air-conditioning roars at full blast. We've just finished an intense game of backgammon when we start talking about our favorite music. He shifts in his seat, reaches behind him for the canvas pouch he always carries, and slides out an old cassette. The melody is unfamiliar, but something in it unsettles me before I even catch the words. When *Sommermorgen* begins, he just leans back. Stilled.

The room fills with sound that cuts straight through me. Mid-verse, I glance at him. He inclines his head, deliberate.

This one matters. We say nothing. We don't need to. This song will become part of the soundtrack of us.

The next morning, he's still asleep, back half-turned to me, one arm under the pillow. I lie there and watch him breathe, and I think: If nothing else lasts, let me keep this. This morning. This stillness. This song.

Wie gern spür ich dich neben mir erwachen. Wie lieb ich dich. "How I love watching you wake beside me. How I love you."

And I Have Kept It

The song stayed with me—too raw for years, yet impossible to forget. Even now, it still brings tears to my eyes when I hear it, because in an instant I am back in that room: him lying there, breathing softly in sleep, and me wishing I could freeze time, just for a little while longer.

I wonder if he ever heard it somewhere and thought of me, even for a moment.

Because I loved him fiercely, and I learned that once you've known love like that, you can't un-know it.

No matter how much you try.

As has become custom, the next morning he drives back into the desert, spends the day at his post, and by evening is on a plane to Cyprus. To her. A visit she deserves and has every right to.

Before he leaves, I don't ask what he's thinking. I'm too busy surviving the ache in my own chest to imagine his. I try not to dwell. But still, the question comes: *Why would fate give me this man—the one I would give everything for—only to remind me, over and over, that I can't keep him?*

I know it can't be easy for him. Leaving like that. Carrying the weight of everything we didn't say. I heard it in the silence before he left, in the things he didn't say. I felt it in the way he held me tighter, in the way he called me "darling", "his Kuwaiti wife." He said it with a twinkle, light and teasing, though I heard the weight beneath. Kuwaiti not by nationality, but by geography. Circumstance. Temporariness. Even now, the phrase folds me in half.

And then, he is gone. Just like that—without drama, without words for what he is leaving behind. The silence is overwhelming, almost too much to bear. I know he can't call, and I try to convince myself not to expect it. But I still wait. Especially now that I have a Kuwaiti cell phone, always charged and within arm's reach. Just in case. Even though I keep telling myself not to.

Ten days without him—can I really manage? I've navigated life solo in the past, but now I find myself yearning for his voice, his touch, the seamless way he integrates into my existence as if it had always been that way. Some nights, I fall apart completely, torn between anger and sorrow. This is the man I could see myself building a future with—if things were different. If timing hadn't worked so cruelly against us, but we met just a moment too late. The pain isn't poetic; it's a tangible ache that coils in my stomach, grips my throat, and hollows out my chest. And it's all because I know—with brutal clarity—that this man is the best thing that has ever happened to me. If we were meant to be, why did timing betray us?

Still, I find myself wondering who truly loses here. She has the title, the home, the legitimacy. What do I have? The longing. The waiting. The nights that end with me lying alone, his scent still clinging to the pillow beside me. Part of me dares to hope that one day, I'll end up on the winning side, the side where love doesn't hide behind silence or excuses. The side where I am chosen, fully and without doubt.

But is that even what I want? And if it is, when will it happen?

A week drifts by. Not a word. Just emptiness.

With Gabby gone, oppressive stillness fills the apartment, echoing my own thoughts back at me. I throw myself into work to escape the silence, yet the weight of the visa applications that pile up on my desk only temporarily distracts me. I stay late at the embassy, stamping passport after passport, hoping that routine will drown out the confusion and pain. My German friends surround me with warmth, offering food, pouring beer, and making space for me at their dinner tables. They sense something is amiss, but they don't pry; they simply offer their presence, which is both comforting and a reminder of what I've lost.

My mind is a battlefield of conflicting emotions. Is he thinking of me? Does he reach for the phone but hesitate, or has he already begun to forget? I'm caught between the hope that he's struggling too and the fear that I was always easier to leave behind. I don't know. I can't know. So I wait—not because I choose to, but because there's nothing else I can do. Not yet.

CHAPTER 7

The Last Exit Ramp

The last few days without him slip by faster than I antici-
pate. My body, racked with flu symptoms, feels heavy and
sluggish. Waves of exhaustion wash over me, pulling me into
long stretches of restless sleep. It is as if my mind erects a
protective barrier, dulling the sharp ache in my heart that
threatens to overwhelm me. Everyday sounds seem distant,
colors muted. I move through the hours slowly, like everything is just a little harder than it should be.

Then he calls, completely out of the blue. No warning—
just his soft, familiar voice slicing through my thoughts,
telling me he's back in Kuwait City. He casually mentions
he'll pick up a few things I might need from the grocery store,
and suggests we'll take a bath together, as if the world hadn't
shifted beneath our feet.

For a fleeting moment, I almost believe it. Everything carries an eerie normalcy, as though he'd never vanished, as
though he hadn't just spent days entangled with his wife, as
though the ache in my chest were nothing but a phantom.

At 4:30 in the afternoon, the door swings open, and joy instantly fills the room. I'm curled on the blue sofa, wrapped in
the familiar blanket, a news show droning in the background
while my mind drifts elsewhere. And then—there he is.
Deeply tanned from the Cyprus sun, a light in his face bright
enough to fill the entire apartment. He moves as if he's never
been gone, his keys landing with a familiar jingle in the bowl
by the door, a bottle of water already in hand from the fridge.
He kneels beside me, kisses me warmly, then slips under the
blanket to guide my feet into his lap. His touch is slow, reassuring, as if we have all the time in the world. My heart lifts

—I've missed him so much, and his touch sends a warm shiver through me.

I don't ask a thing. No questions about what happened while he was away, or if his wife noticed any changes in him. I simply bask in the joy of his presence, cherishing the serene silence between us as something truly special. This is what I've yearned for the most. Not grand gestures. Not longing. Just the sweet simplicity of being together.

Later, he claims his colleagues practically forced him to dinner, so he goes—"just for a bit," he swears. I fight not to take it personally, but it cuts deep. Time now carries the weight of a delicate treasure, too fragile to be shared lightly.

When he returns, having sneaked away early, blaming fatigue, it's as though he never left. He once again collapses beside me on the blue sofa, his knee brushing mine—a tiny touch that anchors something tumultuous within me. We exchange few words, just enough to remember who we are to each other, just enough to feign that all this is normal.

He inquires how I managed without him. I confess that I let the pain take a seat beside me. I didn't chase it away or drown out the silence. I let it exist. I reminded myself that I knew the terms when I chose this path, and I tried my hardest to accept them.

"But something shifted in that silence," I reveal. My memories—once vivid and pulsing with life—began to blur at the edges, lose their sharpness, become dreamlike, as if I'd conjured them from nothing, as if we never existed at all.

Though I don't tell him, I'm reminded of a year ago—a different man, a similar ache. Another UN peacekeeper. Weekends on *The Island*. The salt of the Gulf still on his skin when he kissed me goodnight. Shared time without a future. It really had been, as Marc would later quip, "a deliberate act of charity in a foreign land." We liked each other, but we never fell. That one was easy to leave. Marc isn't. Marc won't be.

When Marc and I first met—long before the first kiss—it felt natural for him to talk about his wife. How they met. Where he proposed. The places they had traveled together, the meals she loved, the future they imagined. I listened easily, the way I once spoke about the man I broke up with in Korea, openly, without guard, as though the past belonged to a different life entirely.

But somewhere along the way, those stories changed shape. They stopped being harmless anecdotes and started carrying weight. During his absence in Cyprus, every imagined detail of her became heavier—her voice in his ear, her face across a dinner table, her body in the bed where I could not be. She was no longer simply his wife; she was the part of his life I couldn't enter, the door I could never open, no matter how close we became.

And so, sitting on my—our—blue sofa with him now, I feel the truth pressing at my chest until it finds its way out. "If you hadn't returned to me, maybe it would've been better. Cleaner."

He gazes at me, startled. "What do you mean?" I have no complete answer. I lower my eyes, a small gesture of surrender, because in truth, I don't want to leave—not yet. Not while we still have time. Not while this fragile love still hovers between us. He insists he doesn't want it to end either. "Then let's pretend we have forever," I say.

I've replayed that evening more times than I can count—how it could have been the moment before everything tipped too far. The last exit ramp we pretended not to see. If we'd parted then, maybe the pain would have been smaller. Maybe we'd have had less to mourn.

But we didn't.

We stayed.

And that choice—to stay when we could've walked away—is the one I would pay for most.

We were at the edge of a cliff, not knowing what was at the bottom —only certain that after we took the leap, nothing would be the same again.

The conversation hangs in the air, unresolved and heavy. We could have avoided the impending wreckage, but of course, we didn't. Instead, we sit there, locked in silence, pretending our choices aren't already cemented in fate.

As the tension mounts, and it's clear neither of us will make a move to leave, we do the inevitable: we drift to the bedroom. Slowly. Wordlessly. He undresses me with deliberate care, as if I'm something fragile, on the verge of shattering. I'm still not well; the risk of him catching it lingers, yet he doesn't hesitate. He kisses me with fierce determination. Makes love to me with unwavering intensity. Midway through, the dam breaks, and the tears flow unchecked. He holds me tightly, unflinching, as everything pours out: the grief that claws at my insides, the relief that floods me, the shame that burns hot, and the overwhelming, impossible joy of having him inside me again.

Afterward, he showers while I lie in bed, staring at the steam rising above the bathroom door. The moment feels like a typical day's end for an average couple, yet unease refuses to let go of me. There's a constant tug within me, a reminder that this semblance of normalcy is just an illusion, and deep down, I know nothing about us is—or ever will be—truly ordinary.

When he returns from the shower, toweling his hair, the steam still clings to him, curling in the air between us. I catch the faint scent of his soap—warm, clean, familiar—and it almost melts me.

The words are already there, though, carried over from weeks ago, from Cyprus, from the long nights when her presence pressed in on me like a shadow I couldn't push away.

"I don't want to hear about her anymore," I say. His hand stills on the towel at his hair, water droplets sliding down his neck. He blinks once, sharply, then says nothing.

It's not that I don't care. It's that I've already heard enough. Once, those details—the small pieces of his other life —felt harmless, almost polite, like two friends exchanging histories. But now they are barbed. I can't step into those memories. I can't sit at that table or walk through that door. I'm torn wanting to know if she's pregnant, what she's cooking, where their adventures will take them, and the futures she envisions, because, deep down, those are dreams I share too. But they're dreams I can't have, at least not with him. Not now, not in this lifetime.

He perches on the edge of the bed across from me, eyes wide and unblinking, as if frozen in place by the weight of what I've just said. I'm not sure he comprehends it all, but I needed to unburden myself. And true to that moment, he never brings her up again.

She was the invisible wound—the ghost in the room. The name unspoken, the face unseen, yet she defined the limits of my love. I didn't have to meet her to feel her presence. She was the boundary I could never cross.

And still, I loved him. Fully. Honestly. Even knowing I'd always stand outside that door.

The following morning, as the sun begins to cast long shadows, he packs his duffel bag. With a soft kiss on my forehead, he heads back to the endless stretch of desert. Back to the nomadic life we share when he isn't with her. The desert is our sanctuary—flat, barren, and wide open—a place where he and I exist fully, in all the ways that truly matter. His wife remains distant, miles away in their home. I stay here, in our oasis.

Yet, as the day ends, the phone rings, a sharp trill slicing through the silence. I freeze. My heart leaps. I lift the receiver, and it's him. His familiar voice pours through the line like a balm, soothing my restless heart. For now, the world settles back into its fragile, borrowed rhythm.

Maybe That's Why I Didn't Fight

Sometimes I wonder why I didn't fight harder for us.

Why I didn't beg him to choose me. Why I didn't ask him to stay.

And the truth is—maybe I already knew he wasn't mine to fight for.

We loved each other. That part was real. But soulmates? I don't think we were.

There was always something missing—not in the feeling, but in the future. I couldn't picture us past the summer. Past Kuwait. Past the fantasy.

He was newly married. I knew that.

And still, I let it happen. I let us happen. But I never once asked him to leave her. I think I knew—even then—that we weren't meant to last.

And that's what makes this bearable now. He wasn't the one. He was the one before the one.

The one who woke me up.

The one who made me ready.

CHAPTER 8

The Ring

The past two weeks since his return from Cyprus have been wonderful. Not flawless—nothing ever is—but rich with presence and warmth. Our love, once fragile, has become more tender. He has always been kind, but now there's a new gentleness about him. It's a softness carrying the shape of an apology, a lingering guilt that doesn't create barriers but reaches out with open arms—gentle touches, prolonged silences, and eyes that seek mine as if pleading for forgiveness without words.

When he undresses me, the moment carries both ceremony and reverence. When he kisses me, I sense the sacredness—the way his mouth lingers as if memorizing me, the reverence in his hands as though I'm something rare. And yet doubt creeps in, veiled but insistent, reminding me that reverence isn't the same as permanence, and that a kiss—no matter how holy it appears in the moment—can't promise a future. And when he holds me, there's a mix of comfort and tension, a space filled with unspoken emotions: the yearning, the pain, and the nagging awareness that this can't last. He moves slowly, not rushing or taking, just being present. I let it happen, of course I do, because I love him, because I miss him when he's not with me, and because I desperately want to believe that tenderness can survive in the midst of such improbability, even though part of me questions it.

Last week, he made up for all the days I spent waiting. He somehow managed to secure an entire week off. Seven days. A lifetime. A gift we never anticipated—and embraced like children.

We spent the day as lovers do. I was fortunate to have a day off work, allowing us to lounge in bed and enjoy a leisurely breakfast without any rush. On the other days, while I worked, he filled the hours with reading, swimming, waiting for me. Always waiting. And when I returned, he was there. We played backgammon on the terrace until the heat drove us indoors. I cooked for him, trying out new recipes and sharing laughs, offering him dishes that were sometimes a success and sometimes not. He was my eager test subject, playfully teasing me with the same gentle voice he uses when he speaks my name.

He chews thoughtfully. "Needs salt." I roll my eyes. "Needs patience." He laughs. "Then I'll wait."

In the evenings, we watched the Soccer World Cup finals —our country's matches, of course—and when the games grew dull, he always found other ways to keep me entertained. He had a talent for inventing positions that made me laugh, made me gasp, made me forget there was a world outside that apartment.

On Friday, after we had lunch, he departed once more, heading back to the camp and his duties. But he assured me it wouldn't be for long. He vowed to return to celebrate my birthday early next week, and he kept that promise.

When the day arrives in the heat of late June, before the evening's dinner, we find ourselves weaving through the gold souk, my favorite place to explore, even though I know none of the items are truly meant for me. The market is vast, a labyrinth of narrow passageways and hidden nooks that seem endless. Its sheer size reflects the importance of gold here in Kuwait, intricately tied to dowries, marriages, and family honor.

We navigate the corridors with the wonder of children, mesmerized by how the bright lights glisten on every polished surface. The heat is oppressive, lingering heavily, mingling with the scents of saffron and warm metal. Everywhere I turn, there's activity—shopkeepers weighing bracelets on small brass scales, women in black abayas gesturing at trays, clerks wrapping purchases in crisp, white paper. Large amounts of cash are exchanged as casually as buying a loaf of bread.

The shops resemble treasure-filled caves, each one brimming with heavy necklaces draped over velvet displays, bangles piled like coins ready to be counted, rings meticulously arranged behind spotless glass. In one of the cases, rows of earrings dangle from a velvet board under a bright light. The designs are exquisite and numerous, each more intricate than the last, with some shaped like flowers, others like coins or tiny lanterns. They resemble miniature chandeliers, delicate and elaborate, far too ornate for any life I've ever envisioned.

While the jewelry designs are indeed exquisite and beautiful, they aren't for me. Those pieces are intended for Kuwaiti and Indian brides, for dowries and family honor. For women whose marriages are publicly declared, celebrated, blessed, and adorned not just with gold, but with significance: status, tradition, belonging.

I reflect on how all these decisions must appear to a bride; each choice a declaration, a promise, something she'll carry into her new life. Here, the brides negotiate their own bridal portions, speaking in low but determined tones, deciding what they'll take into marriage. In my situation, it's the man doing the negotiating while I quietly stand beside him, pretending it doesn't affect me.

I've always preferred the restrained elegance of 18-carat white gold—its soft gleam, its refusal to shout. The brightness of 22-carat yellow gold feels too loud, too insistent; it never suited me. I've never wanted to be seen that way. While I understand why Kuwaiti women buy gold for their dowries, I've always longed for something simpler. Something that didn't need to announce itself.

We'd first seen it a few weeks ago, in the same little shop run by the Indian jeweler who caters to Western women. His designs are lighter, more fluid, a world apart from the heavy, pure-gold pieces most Indian brides favor: rich yellow, elaborate, treasured as much for their purity as their beauty. And there it was, in the case: a white-and-red gold wave curling around itself in a smooth, unbroken line, the two metals meeting and parting like the tide. Modern. Understated. Intimate. It felt like it belonged to us already.

Now we're back to collect it. Marc stands close enough for our arms to brush as the owner, ever gracious, insists on showing us tray after tray of his newest creations. We exchange polite glances, we nod, we admire, knowing we'll take none of them. Marc leans close, his voice low enough for only me. "We already found ours." I nod. "I know."

It's part of the ritual, the polite charade that lends this moment an air of normalcy. And still, under the hum of the shop's air-conditioning, the tragic absurdity presses in: a ring we chose together, a love more all-consuming than anything I've known, and the knowledge that it's already running out of time.

There's a brief ritual of bargaining over the price—Marc acts as the polite negotiator while I pretend indifference, though I already know we will take it. Ultimately, that's all that matters. The shopkeeper carefully places the ring in a black velvet box and slips it into a matching bag. For a moment, I nearly ask Marc to put it on my finger right there in the little shop, but I hold back. Some moments deserve their own special time.

After leaving the souk, we head directly to one of the city's upscale hotels, thanks to an invitation from a friend who's a chef there. That evening seems to belong to a completely different world, with Marc, not just by my side, but truly with me—completely, unmistakably mine, in this place where time bends for us.

We're shown to our table, where a fragrant bouquet in a glass vase awaits us: white peonies and pink roses, my favorite flowers. How he managed to source them in Kuwait is beyond me. Their gentle fragrance envelops us, like something borrowed from another life. Outside, the sky is painted with shades of orange, purple, and pink as the sun sets over downtown Kuwait. The tall buildings sparkle with lights, creating a scene of a bustling metropolis, which Kuwait is not yet. In the distance, the iconic Kuwait Towers rise into the sky, illuminated by spotlights.

Marc assists me into my chair, as any well-trained military officer would, and when I glance up, he's smiling in that unassuming, confident way that makes my heart ache. The pianist in the corner plays another tune, something soft and familiar, filling the space between us.

We appear almost ordinary in our simplicity: I wear black linen dress pants and a crisp white shirt, simple and clean. He is dressed in navy trousers and a similar white shirt, the sleeves rolled just enough to convey relaxation. For the longest time, we are focused solely on each other, tuning out everything else around us, as if the entire room exists solely for this moment.

After the meal consisting of filet mignon, prawns, a fresh salad, he leans back slightly, studying me as if I'm something rare and precious, a treasure he's afraid to mishandle. The pianist's melody drifts between us, wrapping the moment in something soft and unhurried. Then, with that characteristic warmth that always disarms me, he clears his throat.

"I'll be brief," he says, his voice low but steady. "Because you already know this. You are an amazing person, and I hope you never change. Most importantly, I am thankful to have met you."

He pauses, his gaze unwavering.

"The time with you has been a joy."

Another breath, softer now, as his voice falls.

"My only regret is that our paths crossed too late."

He reaches across the table, the linen rustling under his arm, and takes my left hand in both of his. The touch is deliberate, lingering. He lifts the ring from its velvet box and, slowly, slides it onto my finger, his thumb brushing over the metal once it's in place.

"Thank you for being you," he murmurs, the words now barely more than a breath.

My face lights with a joy I couldn't hide if I tried. In that moment, it feels as if there's no past and no future, only this, suspended between us.

The ring signified nothing more than this moment—our shared presence, the here and now. It wasn't a vow of eternal love or a promise of a future. It was just us, suspended in a perfect pause of time.

And yet, when I think back, there is an ache I can't quite name. Part of me wanted more—wanted the story to keep going, to see if it could ever become something solid. But I am grateful, too. Grateful I was never forced to decide whether to fight for us or let it go.

That was the mercy in all of it: the ending was always built in. I never had to choose between my longing and my conscience. The expiration date was set from the start, and all I had to do was live inside the days we were given.

We forgo dessert, agreeing there are better ways to conclude the evening. Since the dinner was alcohol-free, we continue celebrating at my place—with wine, soft music, and an intimacy that doesn't require an audience.

For tonight, that's enough. For tonight, it is as if anything remains within reach.

At the time, I believed I had met the perfect person—the one. However, in hindsight, I realize the truth.

He wasn't the right partner for a lifetime, just for that summer. He suited who I was then: the woman who still thought love could defy consequences. Perhaps that's why it remains unforgettable.

It wasn't meant to endure; it was meant to awaken me.

CHAPTER 9

A Trip to Bahrain

Not long after arriving in Kuwait, I find myself holding onto one dream: driving to Bahrain. Not flying—driving. Not because it's easier, but because it's forbidden. At the time, Saudi Arabia doesn't grant visas to unmarried women, doesn't allow women to drive, and certainly doesn't welcome foreign blondes without headscarves or husbands. That's precisely why I want to go.

I hold a diplomatic passport—a definite advantage. Marc has a service passport—that's helpful too. But to secure a visa, we require a note verbale: a formal embassy-to-embassy request, couched in diplomatic language.

A few days before we're set to leave, I step into the ambassador's office, note verbale and passports in hand, and a well-rehearsed smile.

"Why on earth do you want to drive to Bahrain?" he queries, peering over his glasses.

"Because I'm unmarried," I reply, "and they say I can't."

He raises an eyebrow.

"Then get married."

"I already have someone in mind," I respond confidently, almost too effortlessly. "Just for the duration of the trip."

He laughs. And signs.

A few days later, the passports are returned from the Saudi Embassy—stamped, approved, with diplomatic visas. And just like that, Marc and I are husband and wife. On paper.

If the ambassador only knew, I think. He'd probably find it amusing.

I'm filled with excitement, working extra hours to finish processing the many visa applications from Kuwaitis eager to vacation in my country. It's part of the deal with my col-leagues—finish early, slip away quietly.

Marc and I plan over our daily calls, discussing activities, accommodations, packing essentials, and our departure. I ask colleagues for affordable hotel suggestions and book a room. Marc handles the route from Kuwait to Bahrain. We're both thrilled.

Finally, it's Wednesday afternoon in early July, marking the start of the Kuwaiti weekend. We load the car and head south to the Kuwaiti-Saudi border, passing the familiar ma-rina. Marc is driving, and I'm in the passenger seat. A cassette plays our favorite tunes. No abaya drapes over my shoulders, and no headscarf hides the ponytail at my nape. Instead, I wear a pair of flowing long pants and a simple T-shirt, strik-ing a careful balance between conforming to expectations and maintaining my own sense of freedom.

Even before we reach the Saudi border, the prospect of crossing churns inside me: not excitement, not even dread, just a precise, charged awareness. I check and recheck every-thing—our diplomatic passports, the note verbale with its official stamps, and the ring I wear on my left hand, the one Marc gave me for my birthday.

The car itself has become a capsule of compressed air, thick with unspoken energy. Beside me, Marc's posture is as flawless as if we are under constant surveillance, but there's a flush high on his cheekbones, a dampness at his hairline that the blasting air-conditioning can't quite erase. His hands stay steady on the steering wheel, yet I can feel the heat radiating from him, the kind that has nothing to do with the desert outside.

Outside, the sun bakes the tarmac, shimmering everything into a mirage. We speed south, overtaking a few battered trucks and a family's minivan crammed with children, until finally the landscape swells with low, official buildings, chain-link fences, and the kind of signage that speaks in icons —no cameras, no guns, no dogs, no fun, just leading the way to the Kingdom of Saudi Arabia. The drama of the moment is all on the interior. My throat is dry, my palms slick with sweat, and the cassette (I have swapped it for something wordless and innocuous, Chopin by way of elevator music) plays so softly it is more suggestion than soundtrack.

Somewhere between the last gas station and the main customs plaza, I register a flicker of unease. I do my final sweep of the car: under the seat, in the glove box, behind the sun visors. I have prepared for every contingency—or so I think. Then I see it. Wedged between the emergency kit and the crumpled map of the Arabian peninsula, a magazine lies face-down, glossy pages splayed open. The cover shows a man, shirtless, grinning in a way that would barely register as risqué back home, but in the Kingdom of Saudi Arabia, where the mere suggestion of unveiled femininity or masculine flesh can get you detained, interrogated, or worse, it is a bomb. My heart spikes. I flash through a mental archive of news stories: detentions, border delays, the fate of other Westerners who have misjudged the red lines and ended up in rooms with no clocks and too many one-way mirrors.

I snatch the magazine, my hands moving faster than thought, clawing at the binding. The paper resists, its glossy weight fighting me with every pull. Marc lifts his head, catching the panic written across my face. I tear with no rhythm, no plan, just urgency. The photo. The masthead. The offensive articles. Rip by rip, I reduce them to fragments no bigger than postage stamps. For a flicker of a second, absurdity grips me—a grown woman shredding pulp like a child caught in a tantrum. But then I picture the border inspection, the probing stares, the questions about Western loyalties. And so I keep tearing, until there is nothing left to find.

When I finish, I stuff the scraps into an empty water bottle and twist on the cap. I glance at Marc. He watches the whole performance with a silent, steady gaze, the corner of his mouth lifting in that way he has, amused and impressed at once, as if my crisis management is a small, private magic trick. "Good catch," he says. "You always were good with paper."

We laugh, too loud, the sound bouncing off the windows. The tension loosens slightly, but not all the way. I wipe my sweaty hands on my thighs and try not to think about what else I might have missed. The border is now visible, looming up like a mirage made solid. The checkpoint approaches, a concrete island, a red-and-white barrier pole, and a pair of guards in brown uniforms, slouched in practiced indifference. Marc slows the car. When I hand him the documents, he arranges them in his lap with the precision of a surgeon. I tuck the water bottle deep into my bag, zip it shut, and take a breath.

Marc parks in the designated "Diplomatic" lane, and for a moment we sit in silence, watching the choreography of border life: guards shouting, children crying, an endless ballet of suspicion and routine.

The guard approaches, scanning our plates, then our faces. He is young, with the kind of mustache that seems painted on, and he leans into Marc's window with a practiced authority. "Purpose of visit?" he seems to ask in Arabic, then—seeing Marc's blankness—repeats in English.

"Transit to Bahrain," Marc answers, his accent so neutral it is impossible to place. His voice is even, though up close I can see the fine sheen of sweat along his temple, the tightness in his jaw as he hands over our passports.

The guard thumbs through the pages, pausing at the diplomatic visa stamp. His eyes dart to my left hand, lingering on the gold ring. "You are married?" he asks, a half-smile playing at his lips.

"Na'am." I answer before Marc can. "Yes—we are.

For a moment, everything holds—the thin line between suspicion and acceptance. Then the guard presses the stamp down hard, the ink still damp when he slides our passports back. With a bored flick of his wrist, he waves us through. "Drive safe," he mutters.

As the boom gate lifts, I let out a breath so deep I feel dizzy. "That went well," I whisper.

On the other side, we sit in the car for a full minute, engines running to keep the air-conditioning on, the air thick with relief and disbelief. The desert in front of us presses close, vast and unfamiliar. We turn toward each other, grinning, and then—as if on cue—we both burst out laughing.

Before we drive on, I step out of the car, the heat hitting me like a wall. I pull the magazine shreds from the bottle, one by one, and feed them into the mouth of the tiny stainless-steel trash bin beside us. There's a small, shameful pride in it, the sense that I've not only outwitted the system, but also the version of myself who might have been caught unprepared. When I slide back into my seat, Marc glances over, his gaze softening. "You really want to see Bahrain, don't you?"

I shrug, a teasing glint in my eyes. "I just want to see if I can do it."

His lips curve, but the amusement is edged with something else—a kind of longing, or maybe fear. "You can do anything," he says, almost to himself.

The road stretches ahead—hot, flat, endless. Just sand, sky, and motion. And still, we're buzzing. Talking, laughing. A strange joy rising in the chest. I face each checkpoint calmly. My eyes fall to the ring on my finger, equal parts wonder and disbelief filling me. Calling Marc my husband feels unreal, but it's what the documents say. No one questions us.

The closer we get to the Saudi-Bahrain border, the more I feel it—that wild current of freedom just beyond restriction.

My body hums. Not with fear. With power.

We are defiant.

We are composed.

We are real.

And the signs I'd noticed earlier are now undeniable. The flush is gone from his cheeks, replaced by a feverish pallor. His cough comes more often, each one leaving him shivering despite the blast of the air-conditioning. We'd tried to ignore it when we left, but as the drive progresses, the flu tightens its grip. He holds the steering wheel with both hands, knuckles taut, each breath measured as if to keep going is a matter of will alone.

But he doesn't back out. Not once.

Because this is my dream.

Because I matter.

A weary shadow passes over his face whenever I cast a look over at him, as if to say: *Of course I came. You wanted this.*

I wish I could take the wheel. But I can't—not here. Not as a woman.

So I stay still. And he drives.

Hours pass, but not in silence. Yes, the desert outside is silent—vast and unchanging—but inside the car, we're alive. We go back to talking, laughing, shifting between teasing and tenderness. I hand him water, check his temperature with the back of my hand, fuss over how pale he looks. He tips his head back in mock exasperation but lets me. He's too weak to argue, and too kind to push me away.

Between stretches of laughter and quiet, my glance shifts back to the window. No wonder Western soldiers call this part of Saudi Arabia "the sandbox." It fits. Nothing grows out here. It's just sand and sun and the occasional mirage. But inside the car, we're creating something—a bubble of care, of shared defiance. A small rebellion on four wheels.

Yes, Saudi Arabia is oppressive and surreal, a place never meant to be crossed, only endured.

But we are crossing it.

Together.

He coughs beside me, sweat dripping, breath short. I steady us both, and we keep moving.

And then, finally—after nearly six hours on the road—a shimmer of sea appears in the distance. The causeway. The bridge to Bahrain. And with it, a rush of something I haven't felt in weeks.

Relief.

Bahrain isn't the prize because it's exotic. It's the prize because it's free.

Here, I can exhale.

Here, I can be seen.

Here, for a brief, shimmering stretch of time, we won't have to hide.

Crossing the sixteen-mile long King Fahd Causeway—that long ribbon of road skimming the surface of the sea—is surreal. The border crossing perched on its artificial island doesn't delay us.

This is what I came for. Not Bahrain itself, but the act of crossing.

Of outsmarting.

Of insisting.

Flying is easy. But this… this is the kind of drive you only make once in your life.

And I know—even as we cruise across the causeway—I'll never do it again, so I soak it in. The blue of the Gulf on either side. The glare of the sun. The birds cutting across the horizon like punctuation marks. We're almost free.

By the time we reach Bahrain's capital, Manama, the air feels changed to me—softer, saltier, carrying the hum of a city unafraid of itself.

The hotel we check into is part of an international chain, nothing out of the ordinary, a five-star sanctuary for people like Marc and me, searching for a place to exhale, to escape the stifling Islamic rules of Kuwait that press down on Kuwaitis and foreigners alike.

The pool, so important to relax, is nothing special either—rectangular, tiled, indifferent. To us, it's everything. A small waterfall trickles over sculpted rock, its whisper blocking out the rest of the world. We swim without glancing over our shoulders. We laugh without lowering our voices. We float side by side, legs brushing, suspended in water and time.

Later, we lounge in the shade, towels around our waists, sipping ice-cold beer from dripping bottles. The condensation slides down my fingers, cold and slow.

In Kuwait, this would be unthinkable. Here, it carries the hush of something holy.

This is what freedom can look like.

Drinking without hiding.

Kissing without scanning shadows.

Holding hands without secrecy.

Bahrain itself isn't all that exciting. But here, we can move through the streets without looking over our shoulders. We can linger in a kiss, slow and unhurried, just because we want to. We can laugh too loudly, lean in too close, and no one cares. For two days, we are just a couple, not a secret.

We even start calling it our honeymoon, half in jest, half because it carries all the shape of one. One night, with the warm Gulf breeze drifting through the balcony doors, I sit on the bed brushing out my damp hair after a shower, while he leans against the railing, studying me for a long time as if memorizing the shape of my face.

"What?" I ask, half teasing, though I already know.

He doesn't answer the question. Instead, he says it—the words we both know we can't, and shouldn't, say.

"I love you."

No caveats. No half-measures. Just the truth, naked in the space between us. He says it anyway. And I let it in anyway, feeling it in my chest like something I might never be able to uproot. For a moment, the rules of the world fall away. There is only him, only me, and the soft breath of the air outside, carrying the taste of salt and heat. I don't argue. I don't remind him of what's waiting outside this room. I just let it wash over me, my heart answering before my mouth does.

We go out only once—to the Hard Rock Café, side by side in a dark leather booth, sharing something fried and forgettable. Afterward, we wander the city center, past shuttered shops and glowing signs, the air thick with heat and the faint scent of cardamom. Manama is, at its heart, a souk, a few malls, rows of mosques lit like sentries. But that's not why we're here. We came to breathe. To walk without bracing. To be two people in the open, not a question mark behind closed doors.

We spend the next day playing backgammon by the pool, then wandering down to the hotel's private beach and slipping into the warm Gulf, our legs colliding beneath the surface. We laugh. We kiss. We kiss again.

The second night, we stay in. Room service. TV. Laughter muffled by hotel pillows and soft cotton blankets. We stretch out without urgency, without explanation. He watches me for a long moment, the screen's glow flickering across his face. "Do you ever think about how little time we have?" he asks quietly. I swallow, the question landing where it hurts. "Every minute," I whisper. And still, even in the silence we share, the closeness stays alive. There's no performance. No need to impress. Just warmth, and the ease of being allowed to exist fully, without hiding.

Those carefree days—hours, really—end all too soon. The fever fades. His strength returns. And the spell breaks, as gently as it formed.

We take one last dip in the pool, the morning sun already sharp on the water, and linger over a late breakfast, stretching the hours as far as they will go. Only then do we pack the car, check out, and set off on the long drive back to Kuwait.

The causeway carries us out of Bahrain and into Saudi Arabia, reality pressing in as soon as we cross. From there, the familiar road unwinds before us, broken only by roadside huts where we stop for bathroom breaks.

Somewhere near the border, in the dusty town of Khafji—the last Saudi stop before Kuwait—we pull off for a late lunch in a grim fast-food joint lit by a single flickering bulb. Inside, the air is thick with enforced separation: women on one side, men on the other, families in the center—only if you can prove you belong together.

At the entrance to the family section two guards stand by a metal barrier. They aren't Saudis—probably Pakistani or Indian—hired to enforce someone else's rules. Their uniforms are faded, their faces blank. They don't ask questions. They just inspect our papers, glance at the ring on my finger, and study Marc, who doesn't flinch. Then they wave us through.

We settle into molded plastic chairs under that flickering light, the silence broken only by the fryer's crackle from the back kitchen. Opposite each other, we share fries, cocooned in this surreal fiction. Clusters of women in black sit near-by, veiled and subdued, children fidgeting or nibbling fries at their feet. Some are so fully covered that even their eyes are hidden, so as far as I can tell, the others watch me—not with hostility, but with curious reserve—and catch on the contrast of my uncovered blond hair against their black veils. I meet a few gazes before lowering mine, while Marc sits with practiced composure, careful not to draw attention to himself.

For a moment, all of this is real. We are real. There's no hiding, even in Saudi Arabia. We're allowed to be together. Married, at least for this weekend. He is mine. I am his. No one can tell otherwise, least of all the Saudis.

This is what I came for: to believe we were bending the rules without breaking them. Not with fanfare, just enough to claim our freedom. We arrive back in Kuwait exhilarated. And at last—finally—he is well again.

But freedom has shadows, too. And one of them is a woman I never met. And will never meet.

The Woman I Didn't Know.

What I still don't understand—what baffles me, even now—is how she didn't notice. He was different. He smelled of me. He wore shirts I had chosen, belts I had bought. I would have known the minute he walked through the door. Because love leaves traces—on the skin, in the eyes, in the air.

But I didn't know her. Not her voice, not her scent, not her laugh. She was a fact. A footnote. A name on a form. And yet—she existed.

I told myself I hadn't lied. I hadn't cheated. I hadn't broken anything that wasn't already cracked. But I had been there. I had been the woman her husband chose when no one was watching.

I had hated her. Pitied her. Envied her. I had wondered why she didn't see. Maybe she did. Maybe she just hadn't wanted to know. Just like I hadn't wanted to know what happened when he went home. We had both lived in willful blindness. And he—he had lived two lives.

Only one of us had agreed to that. And it hadn't been her.

CHAPTER 10

Living on Borrowed Time

We return from Bahrain on July 9, the Kuwaiti summer pressing hard, heat rising like a tide around us. Our days blur into one another, yet we fall easily back into a gentle, unhurried rhythm borrowed from a life we can never truly claim as our own, and one we both know is already on a countdown. When Marc is in Kuwait City, he stays with me. We live together in a way that's silently understood, never officially sanctioned, but as real as anything I've ever known.

Sometimes, I come home from work—climbing the two flights of stairs—to find him already there. He's barefoot, engrossed in a magazine from back home, his body perfectly nestled into my blue couch as if it were designed for him. Other times, he's by the stove, humming a tune, setting the table like he's lived there forever. It's as though we're married, simply without the paperwork.

I even managed to get him a key, a small object, but a monumental gesture. And I didn't do it after we had already built a life in those walls. I did it early. Before he left for Cyprus. Before anything was certain. It took navigating the labyrinth of embassy housing protocols, answering probing questions, and filling out endless paperwork. But I persevered, weaving through the red tape without offering any explanations. I just made it happen—because he needed a door to walk through. And I needed the reassurance that he would always have the means to unlock it.

We fall into rituals, quiet and intimate. And with every passing day, the illusion deepens, that this is real, that this is ours, that maybe, somehow, this could last. We share the meals I prepare. I know his preferences for rice and how much salt he likes on his eggs. We sit at the table, our feet touching beneath it. We converse. We laugh. We share intimacy.

Every tenth of the month, he leans in close, his breath warm on my ear, and softly murmurs, "This is the day we fell in love," as if casting a spell that binds us together. His lips meet mine with a lingering kiss, and he draws me into his embrace, whispering the affectionate names he's given me— his darling, his wife, his love—as if they are sweet secrets meant only for us. He drives the exhausting, nearly hundred-mile stretch from the camp to Kuwait City before nightfall— all so he can be by my side. When he's not with me, the phone rings after his long night shifts, his voice heavy and raspy with exhaustion, yet filled with warmth, just to say good morning. "I love you," he tells me, even against the weight of circumstance and the countdown we can't escape, especially in the moments when it is forbidden.

Yet he also pretends. He acts as if there's no end, as if we could pause this moment and return to it someday. I let myself believe it, even though I know the truth: September 30— the date he's scheduled to rotate out and return to his home country—will draw a clear line between what we have and what we can keep.

Some nights, the comforting pretense carries the gentleness of a balm, yet simultaneously, it hurts more than facing the harsh truth ever would. I don't believe his words, but I can't bring myself to silence them either. I want to believe him desperately, because my love for him is undeniable. Deep inside me, there's a flicker of hope, quiet, dangerous, and persistent. Hope for what, exactly, I'm unsure. Maybe it's just the hope to have him for one more day.

Even as I put on this façade, I grasp the reality. I see exactly how this will end, and that's what breaks me. I'm torn, unable to decide what to wish for. Do I want him to stay with me? To choose a life with me over what he has now? To tear apart his current world and build a new one by my side? I don't voice these questions. I never do, because I'm afraid I already know he can't give me an answer.

What Makes a Soulmate?

It's easy to think soulmates are about chemistry. Or timing. Or the way someone makes you feel. But I don't believe that anymore.

A soulmate isn't the person who lights you up for one summer. It's the person who stays lit when the seasons change. It's not just passion—it's presence. Not just wanting you—but choosing you, over and over, when it's hard. When it's boring. When no one's watching.

With Marc, I felt fire. I felt seen. I felt alive. But I never felt safe enough to ask for more. And he never offered it.

That's the difference.

A soulmate makes room for you. Not just in bed, but in life.

He didn't.

Thus, we persist in this illusion. We scrub dishes with soapy sponges until they squeak, fold laundry into neat piles on the bed, argue over the blaring tunes on the radio, and cling to each other tightly under the covers when the world outside is asleep. We are hopelessly naive, yet undeniably alive. Our love burns fiercely, like a flame flickering in the wind, caught between the heat of passion and the chill of uncertainty.

It's one of those nights that slip in easily amid our everyday moments, the kind we'll later fold into memory without worrying over the exact date. Not long after our return from Bahrain, while the heat still presses heavy on the city and our days stretch on borrowed time, I find myself unlocking the door to my embassy building, riding the lingering high of that evening's diplomatic reception at another country's premises, the pulse of music in my veins, the soft clinking of glasses, the buzz of laughter, every head swiveling the moment I arrived wearing that dress. I'd only agreed to come because I had nowhere else to be, because I was sure Marc would be locked down at the camp.

But I chose the dress for myself, too. Short and sleeveless, in a pale green silk that clings just right, skimming daringly above my thighs, just enough to command attention, yet subtle enough for the desert heat and the eyes I longed to provoke. Sexy. Bold. Unapologetic. All because of him, the one who showed me I could own every shade of desire at once.

I step inside, my eyes catching on his desert boots parked in their usual place by the door—dusty for now, though I know he'll polish them before returning to the desert. Keys drop into the bowl, and there he is: still in uniform on the blue sofa, a magazine smuggled from home in his hands, as if he's only just arrived and has been counting every minute for my return. At the doorway, I stop short, my pulse alive with delicious urgency. His gaze sweeps me from head to toe, slow and exact, as though he's drinking me in. Then he rises. I see the quick hitch in his breath, the steady flare of need beneath his composed façade.

A shy laugh slips out of me.

"Grab the camera," I murmur, voice a little husky, pointing to where it rests on the tea table in front of the sofa. "I want a few shots before I change."

I'm not often this made-up—hair teased to a near-cinematic wave, lips glossed just right—but tonight I'm grateful for it, a small tribute to the night he first saw me. That night at the ambassador's soiree, when we shed the pretense of friendship and crossed a line we never looked back from.

He hesitates only long enough for my pulse to thrum through my ears. Then he scoops up the camera. Click. Click. Click.

"Turn around," he says, voice low, taut with something almost feral. I lift my chin and twist, the hem of silk brushing my thighs as I turn. Another rapid succession of clicks. A rush of heat floods through me.

Weeks later, once the film is developed, I'm struck by how utterly unguarded I appear—no pose, no artifice, just a woman wholly alive in her own skin.

He sets the camera down in front of him, as if that little ritual of capture was merely the prologue. Then he crosses the room in a few deliberate strides. My body tenses, knowing exactly what he'll do. This raw current between us—the want, the certainty, the hunger I've never known with another— beats loud and clear.

His hands find the hem of my dress, easing the silk higher with practiced certainty. The charged heat of him presses into my curves, his restraint on the brink of collapse. We hold still, suspended in a breath that tastes of unspent longing, of every stolen moment and whispered promise.

Then he claims me. One hand curls low on my flat stomach, the other on my smooth back, guiding me until my body arches into his. His movements are confident, insistent, a gentle theft, as if he's reclaiming something he's craved from the first moment he saw me.

The inevitability hangs in the air, as though the instant I stepped into that dress I was already his to undress. Neither of us breathes a word. All that remains is the silent accord of desire, the dark promise of what comes next—and the bittersweet sting of the parting déjà vu already gathering in the night around us.

In the weeks that follow, we desperately pretend our stolen moments mean forever, even as I doubt every heartbeat. Whenever he slips back from the desert—sunburnt, dust-covered—we fall into our old rhythm, though part of me bristles at how easily I let him in. In the mornings, his coffee is always strong, mine barely warm. I wonder if the bitterness in my cup betrays my unease. The smallest rituals feel both comforting and vaguely off. Our feet brush beneath the table; silences stretch between sips. They feel like echoes of a life we're borrowing but don't quite belong to.

At night, we cook side by side, flavors mingling and clashing like our emotions. We eat in near darkness, our laughter a fragile shield against the knowledge that nothing lasts. Then we tangle together, craving warmth and fearing what will follow the last ember of desire. We play backgammon for hours, the same worn board laid between us as if those rolling dice could ward off reality. Each clack of a piece carries the weight of a countdown.

The routine seems sacred—muscle memory from a life we once imagined possible—but it's also a knife edge: beautiful and terrifying. Our laughter still sounds like ours, yet beneath it pulses a tremor of dread: time is slipping through our fingers. By late July, I've calculated our expiration date down to sixty-something tortured days. Two months until Marc leaves Kuwait. Two months until this reckless, consuming, tender love must be erased.

I write in my diary: I don't know how I'll survive this. I'm afraid—not just of the end, but of the hollow aftermath. Afraid of waking in a room that still smells like him, only to find it empty. Afraid of reaching for a mug he once held, and recoiling from its coldness. Afraid of hearing "our" song in a café, in a taxi, in a foreign lobby, and dissolving on the spot.

What then? Will I collapse into tears? Will I force a smile I don't feel? Will I flee the room or stay and fracture in silence? I dread the stillness—his silence—when the apartment stops humming with us. I dread the sound of my own breath in the void.

I ache to press pause: to freeze the sunbeam on the floor, the coffee mug half-full, the weight of his hand resting on my hip, the music still playing. I want everything to stay suspended because I don't know how to let go. I vow to savor each second, yet even in our most perfect moments, the haunting tug is there, whispering: you're already losing this.

How do you hold on to something that's already slipping away? I can't imagine being loved like this again. I can't imagine loving like this again, either. Whoever comes after will always be stepping into shadow, always coming after him.

August 7, 1998.

We're in his apartment, the one with the oversized bed that dominates the room, blackout curtains like sentinels guarding us from the oppressive heat and prying eyes, while the air conditioning roars relentlessly, turning the room into an icebox, with a biting cold that makes us forget we're in

Kuwait, a cold that could make us believe the world outside has vanished. But it hasn't. Despite the chill, we find warmth in each other's embrace beneath a heavy, woolen blanket, soon discarded for sheets.

The TV flickers in the corner, its low volume a constant presence, alternating between CNN and BBC. We never turn it off. We're addicted to the news—it's ingrained in us. His uniform. My diplomatic passport. Even off-duty, vigilance is second nature. It's not habit; it's survival.

It's a day I will remember for the rest of my life, not for the sunlight I bask in now, but for the shadow I couldn't yet see.

He's inside me, moving with deliberate slowness. It's an unhurried dance, the kind of lovemaking that is a deep understanding. Nothing rushed, nothing demanded. Just a rhythm we've synchronized to without words. The sheets twist around our legs, my fingers trace patterns on his back. My head tilts slightly to the side, and that's when I hear it.

"Breaking news from East Africa—explosions reported at U.S. embassies in Nairobi and Dar es Salaam…"

I freeze—not from terror, but from recognition. The kind that comes when something too familiar rises to the surface.

The screen bursts with images in harsh green-and-gray chaos: streets littered with glass, bodies wounded and strewn, faces frozen in shock, smoke billowing in thick black clouds. The newscaster drones on—casualty figures, suspected connections, the first images streaming in—but I've already turned my gaze back to him.

Marc's eyes lock onto mine, fierce and unblinking, carrying the weight of a promise. In them, without uttering a word, I hear it: You're safe with me. And then he continues. We both do. We don't stop. Because something inside us already understands: we can't save the world. Not today. All we can do is hold each other tight. And so we do.

Afterward, we lie in stillness. The room is a void except for the soft hiss of cold air through the vents and the distant, looping drone of breaking news. He shifts slightly, reaching for the remote. But he doesn't silence it. He just lowers the volume even more.

We don't speak of what we've seen. We only cling harder, as if our bodies alone could keep the world from breaking in. Outside, chaos spreads. Inside, there is only the sting of cold air, the flicker of a muted screen, and the desperate illusion that for now, for this night, we are untouchable

CHAPTER 11

The Week That Breaks Me

It's August 20—just two weeks before everything unravels, though now I'm blissfully unaware of the impending chaos. Yet, at the same time, every fear I've harbored has somehow manifested. Yesterday, he boarded a flight to Israel to spend a week with his wife. It's not the final goodbye—he'll be back before the month is over—but it carries the ache of a rehearsal for it. And for me, that week would be hell.

The pattern is all too familiar, another conjugal visit marking the calendar, and I can't decide if I should be angry or resigned. Back in June, we still had time together, time that felt almost infinite, wrapped in each other's arms. Now, he's once again whispering sweet promises into her ear, the same ones he once murmured to me in the quiet hours of the night, tracing her skin tenderly as he once did mine. And here I am, coming apart at the seams: silently bleeding from an invisible wound I shouldn't even have.

This isn't just a passing sadness, and I don't know whether to fight it or surrender. It sits with me—constant, unresolved—a weight I carry through the day. I move through the hours like I'm watching someone else live them. Everything feels slightly muted. And underneath it all, the ache doesn't go away. Not yet.

The final days before his departure to Israel were tender and heavy—colored by the knowledge that they were about to end. There was a comfort between us, but also an urgency we didn't name.

We swam in the pool at his building, the one he shared with colleagues but rarely used because he was almost always at my place. The water was already warm from the heat, the surface flickering with sunlight. When we got out, dripping and flushed, we wrapped ourselves in towels and slipped back inside, the cool air of his apartment settling on our damp skin.

We made love like we were running out of time—sometimes slow, sometimes desperate, always as if trying to memorize each other. Afterwards, we would laugh or just lie still, too full to speak, too close to move. Lying there, he brushes my damp hair back from my face. "I don't want to forget this," he murmurs. I rest my hand on his chest, feeling his heart. "You won't," I say, though I'm not sure if I believe it.

Back in my apartment, we ate lunch at the little kitchen table—ripe tomatoes, crusty bread, soft cheese. Simple things, but we treated them like a feast. We passed plates, wiped crumbs off the table, poured cold water into mismatched glasses.

In the afternoons, we collapsed onto the blue sofa, our legs tangled, watching old comedies that made us laugh until we cried. There were long pauses between the jokes, moments when we just held each other's gaze, as if that alone was enough.

At night, we curled into each other beneath the sheets, the room dark and still. We whispered into the stillness—soft things, honest things, the kind of words you only say when everything feels safe. I don't remember what we said. I just remember the feeling, like we were exactly where we were supposed to be.

As the first light of dawn filtered through the curtains, he packed his bags and left for the desert. As the first light of dawn filtered through the curtains, he packed his bags and left for the desert. Standing by the window, I watched his car vanish down the dusty road, my heart breaking with every mile that tore us apart. I knew he would return before long— a brief reprieve in the city—but after that Israel awaited, a distance I could hardly bear to imagine. Standing by the window, I watched his car vanish down the dusty road, my heart breaking with every mile that tore us apart.

Alone in the echoing silence of the apartment, I collapsed. I bypassed the kitchen entirely, ignoring the gnawing hunger that clawed at my stomach. Instead, I sat by the window, chain-smoking cigarette after cigarette, the acrid smoke wrapping around me like a suffocating shroud. Tears cascaded down my cheeks, leaving me gasping for air, yet even his soothing voice on the other end of the phone line that night couldn't reach my despair. It was then that the looming threat over our relationship finally severed the fragile bond we shared.

Gradually, despite our closeness, I had begun to pull away. The endearments that once flowed so easily had caught in my throat. I no longer called him "darling," and "I love you" had become a ghost between us, swallowed by the silence that grew heavier with each unspoken word. My body ached with longing, a constant reminder of the love I would soon have to bury.

Tuesday night, the eve of his departure to Israel, the clock on my bedroom wall ticks louder than it should. The room is dim, and neither of us reaches for the light. We sit in silence, side by side, the weight of what's coming pressing down on everything. Nearly two hours pass—slow, aching hours. I try not to cry, but the tears come anyway. Not from jealousy or suspicion. Just from the knowing.

He's going to see her. His wife. The one he's bound to, even if he's here with me now.

He reaches over, tracing the inside of my forearm with the back of his fingers—slow, careful, familiar. A rhythm he's used before to calm me. Then he pulls me close, wrapping his arms around me like he can shield me from what's next. I let him. Not because it makes anything better, but because I don't know what else to do.

He doesn't say anything. What could he possibly say? "I'm sorry I'm going to see my wife"? Of course not. There's no sentence that softens this kind of leaving.

So we stay there, tangled together in the quiet. His touch is warm. My pain sits in my throat. And everything between us —the closeness, the comfort, the illusion—is already starting to fade.

That night, I lie in bed, hollow and motionless, as he systematically packs his belongings—the crisp new shorts we chose together, the well-worn flip-flops still carrying the sand of Bahrain. My body lies emptied, too frail to rise, with hunger already a distant memory. Each shirt he folds is a small betrayal twisting deeper in my chest; every item lowered into his suitcase chips away at what little resolve I have left. He pauses now and then, offering a tenderness meant to console, but it only sharpens the ache, reminding me he is already leaving.

What must have gone through his mind? Was he agonizing over me while concealing his excitement to be reunited with his wife? He must have suffered, too. But I was so busy sobbing I couldn't see it.

I am consumed by a suffocating sorrow that makes his touch unbearable. When he reaches for me, I turn away—not out of spite, but because my body has become a stranger to me, unable to embrace him while the weight of our impending farewell presses down on me. As I drift into a restless, grief-ridden sleep, I barely notice when he silently slips back under the covers beside me, after relinquishing his car to a colleague.

The light is soft when I wake up. His arms are around me, his breath steady against the back of my neck. I stay still, trying to memorize it—the weight of his body, the warmth of his skin, as if holding on could stop time.

We make love again. Slow. Familiar. Like we're trying to hold onto something that's already slipping away. I cry, though I try not to. For him. For her. For the version of myself that thought I could handle this. Because in just a few hours, he'll be with her. And I'll still be here. Carrying all of this. Sometimes I wonder how he lives with it, this double life. The shifting lines. The stories he has to keep straight.

But mostly I wonder how I do.

Finally, the dreaded moment arrives: I have to let him go. I grip the steering wheel as I drive him to the old school building in downtown Kuwait City, now transformed into a repurposed local United Nations headquarters, known among insiders for one thing: departures. It's the gathering point for personnel before they're whisked away to the airport, and to-day, it's our turn to face the inevitable.

On our way to the pick-up spot, our silence is thick, almost suffocating, like a fog that clings and obscures. I steal a glance at him, a question burning in my mind, but I push it back down. I'm torn, wanting to know if he's excited to see her, yet terrified of his answer. Because I know he is.

Of course he is.

Why wouldn't he long to return to his wife—the woman who carries his name, his promises, his future? The knowl-edge of his excitement knots my stomach. Even if he attempts to hide his true emotions behind a comforting smile, I fear the truth will betray him in the brief pause before he speaks.

The UN building stands desolate, almost ghostlike in the pale morning light filtering through the dusty windows. We clear the security checkpoint as my car rolls into the com-pound, gates lifting with mechanical reluctance before clang-ing shut behind us. A handful of his colleagues linger nearby, engaging in conversation. Some wear the insignia of our own country; others are from across the UN coalition—men from Ghana, Finland, France, Canada—all part of the international force guarding the fragile line between Iraq and Kuwait. Their presence is like an invisible barrier, reminding us that here, in this place, personal truths must be folded into silence.

Marc opens the door and reaches for his bag, the gesture brisk, practiced. For a moment he lingers, his hand brushing mine. I nod. My eyes follow him as he shuffles away.

Having parked the car, I remain a little apart from the group, hiding behind dark sunglasses. My posture is rigid, my hands still, as I perform indifference, pretending he is nothing more than a colleague. Just another officer on his way out. Marc salutes the men, a gesture of duty, of protocol.

I answer with the faintest nod, my own silent salute, invisible to all but me, a private act of loyalty. Yet, in that fleeting moment, I catch it in his eyes—a flicker, a glimpse of the same soul-splitting sorrow that's tearing me apart from within. It's the unbearable weight of goodbye, magnified by the cruel necessity of pretending we mean nothing to each other. He's flying to Israel, to his wife, to the part of his life that doesn't include me. And still, beneath the surface, I know he's tormented too. His chest is probably tight with the same grief that's crushing mine, a silent, shared agony.

He hoists his bag onto his shoulder, giving the briefest tilt of his head that barely masks the turmoil beneath. The shuttle engine roars to life, a mechanical indifference that contrasts sharply with our emotional storm. And then, with a heavy heart, I watch as he steps away, disappearing into the vehicle.

And just like that, he's gone.

In hindsight, I think I already knew I'd have to give him back to her. Not yet. Not fully. But soon.

Something had shifted. Not in what he said, but in what he didn't. In the way he kissed me—gently, like someone already letting go. In the way he touched me—like he was trying to memorize, not to stay.

And I let him. Because I knew he would come back to me. Once more. Maybe twice. But not forever. Never forever.

The drive back to the embassy blurs into a haze of despair, as do the hours I spend at work. I move through the day in a daze, my mind numbed by an all-encompassing heartache. I weep uncontrollably until my coworkers, concerned and powerless to help, send me home. I am a mere shadow of myself, unable to function, with no appetite to speak of, chain-smoking cigarettes and crying until I am emptied of every last tear.

I am slumped on the blue sofa—once ours, now only memory. Its cushions still bear the shape of our closeness, the silence between us now folded into the fabric.

The delicate gold band on my finger catches the afternoon sun, sending a glimmer across the room. It is more than just a ring; it is a testament to our secret, a love that defies boundaries. I think of the day we chose it together in the gold souk, our fingers brushing as we hovered over velvet-lined trays, both of us knowing exactly which one was meant to be ours. I remember my birthday, the soft piano music, the tenderness in his face when he slipped it onto my finger, as if it were the most natural thing in the world.

As I gaze at it now, vivid memories flash through my mind—his warm embrace, the stolen moments filled with laughter, and the whispered promises we dared not speak aloud. The simple design of the ring belies its profound significance, each curve and line echoing the weight of what never could be. A fresh wave of sorrow engulfs me, as this tiny circle serves as a constant reminder of the man who can never be mine and the life we could never share.

Well-meaning people around me keep saying I should cherish the time we had together. I try to heed their counsel: I relive those long afternoons on my blue sofa, making out, reading a magazine or just listening to music, his laughter ringing around us, and the way his eyes locked onto mine as if I were the only person that mattered. But thankfulness doesn't seem to ease the grief. What we shared felt intensely genuine—the thrill of secret whispers, the dread of looming farewells, the hope in stolen moments, the weight of silence. He revealed to me what love should truly be, and losing it is like being erased from existence. Yet, here I am, torn between gratitude for the past and the agony of the present.

CHAPTER 12

The End of Our Summer

September 3, 1998.

The day our summer ended. Not with the slow unwinding we'd imagined, but with a sudden order from somewhere far away, a decision made in a faceless office by people who would never know what it cost us.

It was over. No pause, no half-open goodbye—just the abrupt end. Our love—my love—now existed only in memory, in the ache between heartbeats, in hours I could never reclaim. He'd left an hour ago. For the last time.

By the time he told me, we had only hours left. I had always known our days together were numbered, like sand slipping through an hourglass, but I'd clung to the illusion that we still had weeks before the final grain fell.

Earlier that night, we were tangled in bed, the sheets twisted around us, our clothes scattered across the room in lazy disarray. The air smelled faintly of skin and air-conditioning, of a night not yet surrendered to sleep.

He turned slightly, his face half-buried in the pillow, and whispered, "They're sending me home."

I froze. "What?"

He didn't move. "I didn't want to ruin tonight," he confessed. "But I've known since yesterday."

I sat up, the sheets falling away. "Why didn't you tell me?"

He exhaled, staring at the ceiling as if the plaster might hold an answer.

"Because I didn't know how." He paused. "There's been a schedule change. They're rotating us out early—internal restructuring, they said. Nothing urgent. Just… decided without us."

I stared at him, the finality already settling into my chest. "But we had until the end of September."

"We did. Until yesterday."

He hesitated, the silence thick and heavy. Then, softly, "I didn't want it to end like this either."

That was when I felt the brutal stab of reality beneath the surface, the unplanned finality cutting deep. He had carried this knowledge for a day, maybe longer. I didn't blame him, not truly. I knew he was trying to protect something soft between us. But that delay, that lost window to shape our ending together, made everything sharper. Crueler. There would be no farewell trip to the island. No deliberate unwinding of the life we'd built. Just this: a whispered sentence in the dark, a suitcase already half-packed, and a goodbye arriving days before I was ready. And maybe that's what undid me—not just the leaving, but the suddenness. The violence of having no say. Something in me fractured that night. And the crack only widened from there.

The Scar That Stays

Goodbyes are hard—even when you know they're coming. Even when you've counted the days, rehearsed the exit, told yourself you'll be strong.

Because when love has lived inside you, no amount of preparation can soften the silence that follows. You brace yourself—and still, it breaks you.

That's the thing about real endings: they don't arrive all at once. They seep in, slowly. And then, suddenly, they're everywhere.

His words hung in the air, heavy and laden with a regret neither of us dared to voice. We had pledged—silently, but no less sincerely—to stay together until the end of September.

That vow, cherished and counted on, was abruptly shattered. Snatched away by impersonal forms shuffled in a sterile office, where anonymous officials held the power to dismantle my entire world with the stroke of a pen.

We never got to plan the end. No gentle winding down, no soft rituals of closure. Just an anonymous order and a fixed flight time. I pictured some clerk at a desk back home, shifting a file from one stack to another, unaware that, in doing so, he'd collapsed the most meaningful thing I'd ever known. It wasn't malice. It was bureaucracy. But that made it worse. There was no one to rage at. No enemy. Just a system that moved forward without us.

Three weeks. Twenty-one or so days we had counted on, now ripped from our grasp. And maybe it wasn't just the days I mourned—maybe it was the theft of our agency. The chance to shape our goodbye. To close the chapter with intention, with tenderness. Instead, I was left gasping for air, my heart crushed under the weight of an ending I didn't get to choose.

I never wanted to own him; I only wanted to own the end. When that was ripped away—when the timeline shifted without my consent—something in me broke.

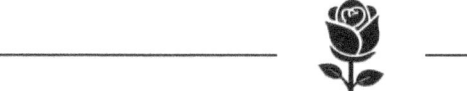

The night before he left Kuwait forever, we engaged in our last, fateful game. We were lounging lazily on the blue sofa, the board between us, familiar yet burdened by an unspoken weight, as if it sensed the gravity of the moment. Silence wrapped around us, each piece moved with a deliberate click, echoing like a clock ticking down to an inevitable end we both dreaded. I emerged victorious—perhaps he allowed it; I dared not question. As the game concluded, he shut the board with finality and tucked it into his bag, his thumb tracing its frayed edge as if etching its memory into his heart. He turned to me then, and in that gaze, I shattered.

I realize, years later, that I've never played backgammon again.

Not once. Not with anyone.

It wasn't a conscious decision. I didn't swear it off. I just... couldn't.

There are some things so tied to a person, they stop existing when that person goes.

For us, it is backgammon. Those slow, silent games. The flick of the dice. His eyes on mine instead of the board. The rhythm we share without needing words.

It's just a game. It's a language. And once he leaves, I forget how to speak it.

He grasped my hands—warm and certain—and for a fleeting moment, it felt like every other night we'd shared. This was the end. A tear escaped before I could restrain it. He didn't release his grip. We sat there, heads bowed, hands entwined, weeping with sorrow, vulnerable, in that raw way when there's nothing left to lose. No grand declarations, no promises, just the aching awareness that what we once had would be lost forever.

When we finally stood, my palms were clammy in his. He held them a moment longer, then gently lifted them to his lips.

We spent one last night together—made love, held each other, drifted into sleep side by side—for the final time. Even then, a part of me knew it would never be like this again. Not with him. Perhaps not with anyone.

The Last Moment

In the morning, I sit on a simple white IKEA chair in the living room. He is kneeling between my knees, holding my hands in his.

We're both sobbing.

This is goodbye—to a summer of love, a summer cruelly cut short by something outside of us. Something neither of us chose.

He's wearing his desert fatigues—the ones I love so much. The ones that made him appear like strength itself. And now they only make this harder.

One last kiss. One last look into those deep blue eyes, filled with anguish.

I trace his face with my fingers, stopping at his lips. Memorizing the shape of them. The softness. The silence. He looks at me, long and full—like he's trying to memorize me, too. Then he reaches up. Gently wipes away my tears. His fingers trail down to my hand, pausing over the ring he gave me, circling it once as if to seal it in memory.

Then, reluctantly, almost reverently, he gets up. He wipes his tears. He reaches into his pocket. And returns the key I once fought to get for him. My key. Our key.

He places it gently on the dining room table. Then turns. And walks away from me, clutching the bag holding the backgammon board.

The door closes behind him.

And just like that—he's gone.

I stayed in that chair for hours, unmoving. The day outside slipped from gold to gray without my noticing. At some point, the light in the room shifted, the thin rectangles from the blinds sliding across the floor, stretching like the hours themselves, but I didn't. I couldn't. My gaze locked on the empty wall in front of me, as if I could stare hard enough to make the door open again, to make him step back inside. My body felt heavy, weighted with something I couldn't put down. My mind was a whiteout, my heart scooped clean, leaving only the echo of where he had been.

How did a person keep living after a love like this? It didn't feel like a breakup. It felt like the end of a world—our world—folding in on itself, vanishing into a place I could never reach. A piece of me had gone with him, and I already knew it wasn't coming back.

I tried to remind myself that heartbreak was universal. People endured it every day. They cried, they healed, they found new love. But this was different. This wasn't ordinary. This was rare, once-in-a-lifetime rare, the kind of connection you couldn't replace with someone "nice" or "good for you." And now it was gone, ripped from me with no warning. I couldn't imagine ever experiencing that again, the fullness, the fire, the way he saw me as if no one else existed.

And maybe I'd felt it coming. Even before he returned from Israel, there had been a shift, a shadow I tried to ignore. This was the final act, the beginning of the end, the packing-up of a love story and shipping it home in a box marked "finished." The agony—the chain-smoking, the tears that left salt stains on my skin—hadn't started that morning. It had been brewing for weeks, low and steady, waiting for the final blow.

And still, he had wept as he left. That was what haunted me—the tears streaming down his face, cutting through all the rules, all the pretenses. Because he had loved me. Fiercely. And I had loved him with everything I had, the kind of love that burns you and leaves its mark forever.

I glanced at my watch. By now, he was already gone—past the tarmac, past the city, past me. The thought gutted me: my appetite vanished, sleep came only in scraps. Tears arrived without warning, sudden and unstoppable, leaving me hollow in their wake. The pain sat heavy, pressing into my chest like an anchor, a shadow I knew I'd carry.

It was a private suffering, one that couldn't be confessed to friends, not really. They would have listened, of course, and offered gentle commiseration. They would have said all the right things—"this too shall pass," "you are so strong," "there will be other loves"—but I knew, even as I went through the motions, that this particular pain was mine alone. It was the cost of loving someone without reservation, the tax paid for joy that had once seemed infinite.

I couldn't hate him for leaving me, because I knew he hadn't *wanted* to. He didn't walk away. He was pulled. And I couldn't hate myself either, because this wasn't about not being enough. It was about the inevitability we had both accepted from the start. Ours was a love with a time limit, a season we had chosen to live fully, knowing it would end. There was only the ache, and the knowledge that it was both my punishment and my privilege for having loved—and for having been loved—so fiercely.

I couldn't believe I would ever know those emotions again —the love, the way he saw me. The thought of trying to replicate it felt unimaginable. How do you move forward when your present leaves, taking everything that matters with it? He hadn't meant to break me—I know that. But the damage was done. He had boarded a flight, three weeks earlier than we had planned. And I wasn't even angry at him, only at the faceless machinery that had made the decision for us. Three weeks. Taken. Not out of necessity, not for war or crisis, but because someone back home had shifted a line on a schedule. That's what undid me. The banality of it. The absolute indifference to what we had shared.

The following days I found myself in a constant struggle with food, sometimes picking at my meals, only to shove the plate away still half-full. The nights were restless, filled with tossing and turning as I stared at the ceiling, willing sleep to come, but dreading the dreams that might follow. Tears often ran down my face without warning, catching me off guard, while moments that should have broken my heart instead left me numb and hollow.

The ring remained on my finger, a small, but heavy reminder of what had been, and I couldn't decide if I wanted to cherish it or cast it away. The silence around me was suffocating, pressing in like a fog I couldn't escape. I felt like a fragile shell—brittle and ready to crack—yet there was a part of me that longed to be strong. The pain was a constant shadow, an unshakable burden I feared I'd carry forever. My silent tears carved paths down my cheeks, leaving an ache that resonated from deep within, and I was torn between embracing the sorrow and fighting for a semblance of peace.

I longed to roam my apartment like a caged creature, yet there I was, anchored to my blue sofa that held a lifetime of memories. My eyes were fixed blankly on the wall as the ashtray continued to fill. Each attempt to move, to speak, or even to merely be, was met with a rebellion from within, my body quaked, felt nauseous, and empty. I yearned for motion, but I was paralyzed by my own contradictions.

The only solace I had then was that I was finally forced to recognize my unnamed depression—the heavy burden I had carried for years without realizing what it was. Marc's departure had ripped away the veil, exposing the darkness. The decision came like a cold wave in the middle of a sleepless night: I needed help. Not a walk, not wine, not another call with someone who meant well but didn't really understand. I needed somewhere I didn't have to pretend. And though I wasn't alone in the world, I was still the one carrying myself out.

After a few more days of wrestling with the weight, I mustered the courage to reach out. I dialed my doctor back home, a familiar voice who had seen me through past struggles and knew the signs all too well.

The words caught in my throat, but I managed to say, "I need help."

He hadn't hesitated, his voice calm and steady as he arranged for a hospital bed without delay. Where I'm from, you don't need to be suicidal to be hospital-admitted. Just visibly crumbling—and brave enough to say it out loud. In my country, we name pain. In Kuwait, you endure it.

But in a way, I was still doing this alone. That had always been my strength: even when engulfed in my darkest moments, wrapped in a blanket of deep sorrow, I had possessed the ability to find the path to save myself.

The unraveling was intentional. I wasn't falling apart by accident—I was choosing to let go. Choosing something different. A place with harsh lights and narrow beds. A place where I didn't have to pretend. A place where vulnerability wasn't a weakness, but the only way forward. And that was what I clung to: even when everything else had deserted me, I hadn't deserted myself.

My colleagues at work listened sympathetically as I explained my urgent need to leave the country, their faces carrying a mix of concern and unspoken questions. They offered me gentle pats on the back, gestures meant to reassure, signaling their respect for my privacy. Beneath their surface kindness, I could almost hear the unspoken verdict: *She shouldn't have fallen for a married man.* And yet, when has the heart ever bowed to reason?

A week after Marc's departure, I booked my flight. I packed slowly, each fold deliberate, as if smoothing the wrinkles in my clothes might smooth something inside me, too. When I zipped the suitcase shut, I placed one hand on its textured surface and the other over my chest. "I'm not falling apart," I whispered. "I'm not falling apart." My voice wavered. I wasn't sure I believed it.

At the airport, the air-conditioning rose harshly from the polished floor, the kind of manufactured chill that seeps through shoes and straight into bone. It felt less like cool relief than a reminder of absence. My legs were leaden, each step a monumental effort. I was too weak to walk the endless corridors. A caddy approached, his uniform crisp and a polite smile in place, offering assistance. I nodded, grateful, and he maneuvered me to the departure gate with professional efficiency, his presence a gentle reassurance. I sat back in the cart, too drained to resist the pull of exhaustion. There was no fight left in me, only the decision to move forward.

As the plane lifted from the runway and began its slow climb, I let myself lean into the transformation, the shift from a world I had loved to one I had to leave behind. I carried the joyful moments with me: the laughter, the way Marc had made me feel singular and seen. I remembered the shared meals, the sun-drenched island afternoons, the lazy mornings draped in music and light, wrapped in a closeness that had once felt unbreakable. I held onto the happiness, the comfort, the love that had seemed eternal, and in doing so, I set down the pain, the exhaustion, the simmering anger I had once aimed at him, at myself, at the audacity of loving someone I was never meant to keep.

Below me, the Kuwait Towers gleamed in the afternoon light, standing tall and unshaken as they had through all our days there, their blue spheres catching the sun one last time before fading into distance. The engines hummed with promise as the city's glitter slipped away, dissolving into the vast, unbroken desert, the world below reshaping itself into a canvas of change.

I knew I would return. But for now, I allowed myself this small surrender, a single, steady breath in which the ache and the beginnings of something new lived side by side.

CHAPTER 13

Requiem and Return

Today would have been our five-month anniversary. Anniversary. The word implies years. But we never got a year, barely even months. Just a few precious weeks, days really. Barely a handful of tenth-of-the-months, quietly noted, quietly cherished. And still, we made the most of them.

I try to push it all away, but the flashbacks come without warning.

Five months since we first made love. Already it carries the weight of a lifetime ago.

The flick of his lighter in the dark.

The smell of his aftershave lingering on my pillow.

The way his fingertips traced slow circles on my arm, as if touch alone were enough.

The sound of his voice calling me darling in the stillness between sleep and waking.

The clink of backgammon pieces late at night, his foot pressed lightly against mine under the table.

The glint of gold from the ring he slid onto my finger—not in ceremony, but in something that felt deeper.

The flashbacks still hurt, a requiem for a love that would not return.

And yet, thanks to the medication, I manage to stay afloat —for now. What it will be like when I return to Kuwait—to my apartment, the one that holds every memory of us—I don't know. I'm afraid to find out.

At this moment, I'm still confined—to this hospital room, to the slow and disorienting process of healing, and to the quiet reckoning of having to face myself. In essence, I am alone. My mother is here, but at a distance—partly hers, partly mine. I hadn't told friends here at home either; there weren't many to begin with, and even those I kept at arm's length, another hidden cost of a childhood spent moving from place to place.

The antiseptic scent clings to the air as I lie on the stiff, white sheets, my mind a turbulent sea of suffocating anxiety. Waves of deep sadness wash over me, and a hollow ache throbs in my chest as I stare at the sterile ceiling tiles. My thoughts circle endlessly, questioning if I'll ever truly move past the memories of him. But beneath the heartbreak lies something older: the lifelong anguish of loss I never dared name. The unresolved, recurring trauma of being moved, again and again, across borders and time zones, learning not to hold on too tightly—until him. Beneath the grief lies a subdued anger—not at him, never at him, but at the circumstance. At the years of constant uprooting that weren't mine to choose, at the way impermanence was woven into my childhood, and at how helpless I felt when it came for love too.

The First Anchor

Marc was the first man I ever truly loved.

Not admired. Not desired. Not simply grown attached to.

Loved—in the full, breathtaking, terrifying sense of the word.

Until then, I had lived in motion. Countries changed. Friends faded. Goodbyes were the only constant.

I learned how to float through it all—self-contained, composed, untethered.

I didn't expect more. I didn't ask for more.

But he gave it anyway.

He saw me. Wanted me. Held me.

And for the first time in my life, I felt what it meant to be chosen. Not out of convenience or timing—but with clarity.

With certainty.

He became my first anchor. Not because I needed one. But because I had never known what it felt like to rest.

And when he was taken from me—not by cruelty, but by the indifferent machinery of duty—I came undone.

It wasn't just the end of a love story.

It was the end of a gravity I had just begun to trust.

Restlessly moving through the hallway outside my room, I wonder if it would've happened anywhere else. If we hadn't been in Kuwait.

In Another Life

Sometimes I wonder if it would've happened at all—if we'd met back home, surrounded by people who knew us. There would've been expectations. Boundaries. A hundred watchful eyes waiting.

But Kuwait was different. The heat softened everything. The silence rearranged the moral lines. We were far from home, far from consequence. And with his wife so distant—not just in geography, but in presence—the line between what was permitted and what was desired faded more easily than either of us expected.

In another place, in another life, maybe we wouldn't have crossed that line. Maybe we wouldn't have come close. Maybe we would've remained polite colleagues with fleeting tension and a handful of shared smiles.

But Kuwait made space for the impossible.

Not inevitable. Just possible.

In the meantime, I do what I can. Some mornings, the most I manage is peeling back the heavy duvet and swinging my legs over the side of the bed, feeling the cool floor beneath my feet. On better days, I venture out for a walk, letting the crisp air fill my lungs and the soft rustle of fallen leaves accompany my steps. I eat a little more each day. Nothing dramatic. A slice of toast. A spoonful of soup. But it's something. My body is learning safety again. Sometimes, I engage in a heartfelt conversation or a cigarette with a fellow patient or nurse, finding solace in shared words and understanding. On rare occasions, a genuine laugh escapes me, surprising and uplifting in its spontaneity.

I gently remind myself to ease into the moment, taking deep breaths while nestled in the comfy armchair just outside my room, a warm cup of chamomile tea resting in my hands. I embrace the slow, steady pace of my progress, observing how each day contributes another small stone to the path I am crafting.

I tell myself to be forgiving and patient as I leaf through the journal entries that map my journey to and from Marc. On the page, I see the ache and the unraveling, but also the first fragile steps away from it. Healing has its own pace—not fast, not dramatic, but steady. Each day nudges me a little further from where I was.

I'm grateful that no one pressures me to hurry as I move through my days with a gentle rhythm. Each day is punctuated by therapy sessions in a cozy, softly lit room where I sit on a cushioned chair, sharing my tangled thoughts with a therapist who listens intently, her eyes kind and patient. Beyond those structured hours, the day stretches before me like a blank canvas, mine to fill as I choose.

I am granted something rare in settings like this: the freedom to come and go as I please, a precious gift not everyone here enjoys. My doctor, with his perceptive understanding, knows that the sun's warmth on my skin and seeing the expanse of open sky above are essential elements of my healing process.

It takes nearly a week of therapy before I'm ready to step out into the world. I wander down the cobblestone streets, past quaint bookstores with their colorful window displays and inviting bakeries where the scent of fresh pastries wafts through the air. The late-summer sun casts a golden glow, warming my face and shoulders. I breathe deeply, taking in the mingled aroma of bustling traffic, floral perfumes, and the mouthwatering scent of freshly baked bread. And for a few fleeting moments, as I stand amidst the vibrant life around me, I can almost believe I am alive again.

One afternoon, Marc and I meet outside the hospital—a quiet corner near the main entrance, where the traffic drifts past like a restless tide and no one takes notice. He's the one who calls, his voice warm but softer than I expect, saying he wants to check on me. Just to see how I'm doing.

Back home, we both live in the capital. I still keep my apartment here, but the hospital is a world apart from ordinary life, and he's carved out a sliver of his evening to step into it. For a moment, in this small pocket of time, the world has narrowed to the two of us again.

We move to a tall oak tree, its branches reaching wide overhead. He tells me about the internal restructuring that brought him back, the decision made far above either of us, the one that cut his posting short and ended everything we had. I listen, absorbing his words in silence. Then it's my turn to tell him about therapy, not the hard parts, just enough to say I'm trying. That things are steadier now. Most days.

When he smiles, I see it—that same glint, that flash of light that once made everything else fade.

"You look better," he says, hands tucked into his jacket pockets.

"Most days, I'm just pretending."

He doesn't argue. He just watches me for a moment, the way he always used to. But this time, I don't come undone. I don't sense the old pull. Just a delicate shift inside me. A kind of sigh I didn't realize I was holding.

It's not that I stopped loving him. I still do. Maybe I always will. But I know, now, that it's time to let go of something I never had.

And it's not just about Marc. It's the years before him. The unspoken grief. The sense that life kept moving while I stayed still. Losing him wasn't the whole story. It was simply the last break in something that was already starting to crack.

This heartbreak has brought everything bubbling to the surface, like a pot left too long on the stove. Now, it's impossible to turn a blind eye—not my family with their well-meaning advice, not those who check in with gentle concern, and certainly not me as I lie awake at night, staring at the ceiling.

While I'm profoundly grateful for the unwavering support from my colleagues at the embassy, my family's persistent check-ins, and the few friends I have kept over the years who have been my lifeline through it all, there's a part of me that is starting get excited about returning to Kuwait, the place I currently call home, with its bustling streets and vibrant sunsets.

As much as I dread being engulfed by the memories Marc and I created, I yearn for the comforting familiarity of my own home. The rich aroma of my favorite Colombian coffee that wafts through the air each morning, promising a fresh start, when I sink into the worn texture of my blue couch, its fabric soft against my skin, as the gentle hum of the city filters through the windows. The predictability of my life, with its small and comforting rituals, waits patiently for me there, offering solace amidst the chaos of my thoughts.

I whisper to myself that one day I'll reminisce about all this with warmth, that I'll remember Marc without the sting of regret. I tell myself I'll love again, not with the guarded caution or timid hesitance that fear breeds, but with the same fierce intensity and boundless passion I once felt for him. Anything less would betray the depth of what I now understand love to be.

Still, life has a way of testing that resolve. He called again yesterday, his voice familiar yet distant as he casually asked how I was doing. It was a thoughtful gesture, one that once would have sent my heart into a flurry of emotions. But this time, I felt little more than a serene stillness, no ache, no spark, just a resigned acceptance. Maybe I've already begun to let go. Unbeknownst to me, it would be the last time we spoke from inside that version of our lives.

Yet I remain in survival mode, constantly on edge as if bracing for an unseen danger. My therapist and I sit across from each other in her warmly lit office, surrounded by plants and the scent of lavender. We agree that the only way to heal from Marc's abrupt departure and the shattering end of our sunlit summer dreams is to let him die—not in body, of course, but in memory, in presence, in routine.

"I need to mourn him," I tell her, my voice barely audible. "But there's no funeral. No grave. Just… absence."

She doesn't speak right away. She simply anchors me with her stillness. "It was never going to be permanent," she says gently. "But some things don't need permanence to leave a mark. We grieve them anyway."

I look down at my hands, then back at her. Not because it fixes anything, but because it is the first time someone gives me permission to grieve what no one else can see. Including the part I don't say out loud yet—that mourning him will one day mean taking off the ring.

Not here. Not yet. But soon. Because how do you say goodbye to something that once felt like everything? Perhaps it begins with loosening my grip: our shared moments, the kind that fill rooms with laughter echoing off the walls during endless evenings, the tender closeness as we walk side by side through the sparkly gold souk, our fingers never touching but always aware. It is time to bury the "us" that once ignited my life with a fiery passion, that made my heart race with a joy so intense it felt like flying.

Grieving a man who still walks the earth is a peculiar kind of sorrow. The ache is real, but invisible. There are no announcements, no ceremonies, no language for this kind of loss. In Kuwait, we were seen. But here, it is just me, alone in a room, holding a love that cannot be acknowledged—not to my mother, not to my friends, not to anyone —a silence edged with shame. Carrying a goodbye that was real, but never the one we had hoped for.

Maybe that is what makes it harder. I am not just grieving the man. I am grieving the intimacy, the small rituals, the version of myself that exists only with him. Is it a fantasy? Perhaps. It was never going to end well. But that doesn't make it less true. I haven't lost a future. I have lost a moment—blazing, unrepeatable, irreplaceable. And it has opened something in me that will never fully close again.

And part of that decision—the hardest part—is coming to terms with the fact that I will no longer see him. No more messages buzzing through with a sharp beep. No more late-night calls bridging the distance between us. No more whisperings of *"Ich hab dich lieb"* in the dark. No more games of backgammon, no more stolen smiles across a room that never dares to see us as us. No trace of his existence woven into the fabric of my daily life.

That is the price of loving with wild abandon—and of being loved with an intensity that leaves no room for middle ground. Letting go isn't just painful. It is excruciating. And in that silence, I convince myself it has to be irrevocable, a decision as immovable as a mountain.

And it is.

Until one day—twenty-five years later—I realize it doesn't have to be final after all.

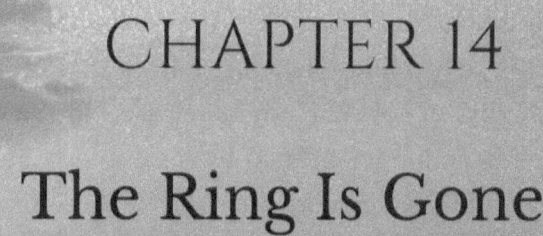

CHAPTER 14

The Ring Is Gone

Three weeks after I was admitted, I'm discharged. No fanfare, just plain consensus that I'm ready. Not fully healed, but ready to try.

The suitcase lies open on the bed in my apartment, each item folded with deliberate precision, as if I'm packing away a different part of myself with every layer. I'm going back to Kuwait, to the life I left hanging in midair. A crisp white blouse rests beneath my palms. I smooth it flat, then reach for a tube of mascara I haven't touched in weeks.

The small, deliberate strokes are foreign yet strangely invigorating. In the hospital, with its sterile walls and absence of mirrors, beauty had felt pointless; survival was all that mattered. But here, in front of my bedroom mirror, I'm ready to see myself again, or maybe meet someone new, a woman claiming her place in the world for the first time.

The mirror stirs a faint memory of another night, another mirror—Marc's reflection beside mine as I adjusted an earring, his presence warm, steady, a comfort I didn't know I'd miss so much. Back then, I leaned on his gaze. Now, the reflection is only mine. The ring still gleams on my finger, a trace of him I'm not yet ready to release, but the woman looking back is no longer defined by his absence. She is learning to carry both—his memory and her own becoming.

My hair falls in loose waves as I undo its tight hold with blond strands cascading down my back like something long forgotten. Foreign yet liberating, it affirms—silently—my readiness to be seen once more. The leather boots I choose are well-worn, their scuffed soles and resilient stitching declaring: I'm still standing strong. With a decisive motion, I zip the suitcase closed, sealing away not only my clothes but also my lingering affection for Marc. Though not vanished, it is neatly tucked away, resting in its own secluded corner.

At the airport, a passport officer flips through my documents without acknowledging me. This time, I don't need a caddy to guide me through the corridors; my legs carry me on their own. Shoulders squared, I approach the departure gate with a trace of nostalgia softening my face. Later, on the plane, a flight attendant offers me a small plastic cup of water. I thank her with a faint nod. A couple nearby argues in hushed tones over their seat assignments. All around, passengers shuffle newspapers, adjust their seats, and speak in a myriad of languages. None of them realize the significance of this journey to me. To them, I am just another traveler who showed up despite everything.

I have no idea what the future holds, but, for the first time in a long while, hope flickers softly within me. One thing is clear: I remain resilient and upright. I've loved wholeheartedly, savoring each moment without needing promises. I've encountered loss and survived it. Amidst the chaos, I discovered a part of myself I can rely on. The journey ahead will be lengthy, but I've come this far, and I'm prepared to start anew.

As the plane lifts gently from the runway, I lean back into my seat, watching the city shrink beneath me. I am headed back to Kuwait—to the place where it all began, where I now choose to begin again... and eventually come full circle.

Hours later, as we begin our descent, the vast desert unfurls below us, a sunbaked expanse of endless beige stretching to the horizon, yet somehow familiar in its stark simplicity. I step onto the tarmac, and the familiar late-summer heat engulfs me like a wall, heavy with warmth and humidity, impossible to escape yet strangely welcome. Instantly, my hair responds to the humidity, spiraling into curls, but I remain unfazed. I draw in a deep breath, the sharp tang of jet fuel mingling with the omnipresent dust.

Inside the arrivals hall, the ever-present, familiar symphony of languages—Arabic, Hindi, Urdu—swirls around me, vibrant and pulsating with energy, a world apart from the quiet tones of home. And I exhale, not out of nostalgia, but relief.

A few days pass before I return to work—days spent savoring the tranquility. With school in Kuwait back in session and travel season over, my caseload is mercifully light, and my colleagues tread carefully around me, sparing me from intrusive questions. One of them begins to ask if I'm okay but halts abruptly, as if sensing that the inquiry alone might shatter my fragile composure. I give the slightest sign of thanks, and we leave it at that. They understand I've been through a personal turmoil, and they respect my privacy.

Familiar routines return slowly: sheets already clean get washed again, the fridge fills with olives, apricots, and that sweet juice Marc always turned his nose up at. During the day, I still have to keep the windows shut, the outside air too stifling to bear, and I skip my usual walks due to the oppressive heat. But as night falls and the air becomes cooler, I step onto the terrace. The city below is a chorus of everyday life—cars whizzing by, the distant call of muezzins from the mosques, the steady drone of air conditioners. I light a candle, the same kind he used to light during our backgammon games beneath the stars. It's not to conjure his presence or to indulge in fantasies, just a plain acknowledgment that I'm here. Still here. Breathing in. Breathing out.

Soon after, I resume therapy in a plain beige office near the marina. I speak more slowly than before and listen to myself more than I ever have. We talk about grief, about silence, about clinging to things long after they've passed.

"Do you still want to wear that?" my therapist asks gently, gesturing toward my hand.

The weight of the ring returns to my awareness—once so familiar, it had nearly faded into the background. It sparkles in the warm glow of the afternoon sun, drawing my attention.

That evening, I wistfully stare at it, recalling the moment he gently placed it on my finger. It was after dinner, and his gentle gaze made everything feel right—just us, no secrets, no fear.

But that version of us has closed.

Standing by my bed, I take a deep breath and slip the ring off, not out of sadness or bitterness, but with a clear understanding: this love has been a part of my journey, yet it no longer fits the woman I am becoming. I tuck it safely away in a drawer and move forward with my evening.

The Ring is Gone

I had it melted.

Years later, with intention and subtlety, I crafted it into something new.

A different piece of jewelry, devoid of any recognizable past. The ring fulfilled its role and was no longer a part of my present. I still wear it, though not as a ring.

This is how healing unfolds—not by erasing the past or reinventing oneself, but by staying present with the pain until it gradually eases. I welcome the memories, let them sting, and then let them settle.

I know Marc will always have a place in my heart. One day, I will open my heart to someone new, completely and wholeheartedly. That day will arrive, not in spite of this love, but because it has prepared me for it.

My journey isn't over. I have loved and been loved. Now I am ready for my last love.

CHAPTER 15

The Man Who Stays

Fourteen months after Marc and I were forced apart by circumstances beyond our control, I crossed paths with the man who would eventually become my husband. I wasn't searching for love. But I can't deny I was hoping for it.

Once you've experienced real love, the kind that pulls you into full alignment, the kind that leaves you changed, it's hard not to ache for it again. Love doesn't just imprint the heart; it leaves a silence behind, and sometimes, even that silence is longing.

At the time, I was still caught in something vague, a relationship that flickered on and off, held together more by inertia than feeling. It wasn't serious. It wasn't love. It was just... not quite over.

And then came Nick.

It was a balmy late November night in a lively Kuwait City. The newest group of military officers from my homeland had just arrived, prompting the usual welcome party at the apartment rented for their stays in the city. This apartment wasn't the same one where Marc had lived with his fellow officers; this one was conveniently located above the home of my German friends. That closeness led to frequent gatherings, where wine was plentiful, food was abundant, and laughter filled the warm, slightly humid air. Inside, the air conditioner had been turned off for once. Only a ceiling fan stirred the warm air, and the occasional current of air slipping in from the courtyard. It was one of those nights when the heat didn't press down anymore but seemed to hang gently around us, as if even the weather knew how to hold its breath.

The party was already in full swing when I arrived with a large bowl of salad wrapped in cling film, a bottle of wine nestled in the crook of my arm, and no particular expectation. My mind was elsewhere: work, errands, fatigue. I walked in, set the food down on the crowded table, masking exhaustion with a few quick pleasantries, and sank into the nearest sofa.

A moment later, Nick sat down beside me.

Not too close. Not performative. Just there—companionable, easy. As if it was the most natural place for him to be.

Someone handed me a cold beer, nothing fancy, just familiar and refreshing. I took a sip, then turned slightly to face him. He was already holding a glass of white wine, the condensation pooling at his fingertips.

He raised it toward me, amusement flickering in his voice. "To surviving another rotation."

I lifted my bottle. "To cold beer in warm places."

Our glasses met with a soft clink. No spark. No sizzle. Just… something. Grounded. Present. Real.

"You're with the observers?" I inquired.

He nodded. "Just arrived last week. Short tour. I'm a medical student. This helps pay the bills."

"So medicine first, army second?" I challenged.

He gave a small shrug. "Depends on the day. I'm already trained as an observer, but I'm not full-time military. Yet."

"Yet," I repeated, amused. "That sounds like a plan in progress."

He smiled. "Something like that."

The exchange wasn't flirty. It wasn't trying. It was simply two people, sharing the same couch and the same air, enjoying a pause neither of us had planned for. I didn't think much of it at the time. But I didn't move away either.

As I'd done many times before, I invited him for dinner. Nothing more than kindness. Nothing with intention. Just a friendly gesture in a long string of ordinary days.

He showed up right on time, as I knew he would. Clean-shaven, slightly flushed from the walk across the compound, his shirt lightly creased, hands empty, which made perfect sense. He didn't need to bring anything. My cupboards were always stocked, the wine already chilled, the meal already planned. It wasn't about impressing. It was just... easy.

Our conversation picked up right where it had left off, as if no time had passed. There was something unhurried about him. He made space, without trying to fill it.

I served roasted vegetables and something vaguely Mediterranean, likely chicken with lemon. The kind of dinner that could stretch or shrink depending on the conversation. We ate slowly, the light outside fading as we talked. The windows were cracked open, and the faint sound of someone watering plants in the courtyard drifted in.

And when he left, the familiar ache was absent, the tug of something unfinished, the solitary grief that usually followed small goodbyes. I closed the door behind him and thought: That was good.

And I wanted to do it again.

We didn't speak every day after that. Not yet. But the next time he came into the city, he called. A real call—landline to landline. Just the sound of a phone ringing, and then his voice on the other end. Calm. Like it had always been there, waiting.

That's how we, the us, began. Not with a grand moment, but with a thread. Quiet. Slowly forming.

We saw each other once more before the holidays—lunch at a friend's, a group gathering. Nothing private. But I was glad he was there. And once, across the table, I caught him watching me. Not in a way that unsettled me, but in a way that said: I see you. I'm paying attention. I broke eye contact, then returned. He hadn't. He was still watching.

December came quickly. I booked my flight home, not for winter, but for Christmas. For the usual traditions: the crowded dinners, the candlelit services, the comfort of being surrounded by people who had always known me. My family. He asked when I'd be back, and I told him. No agenda. No pressure. I wanted him to know. We didn't make promises. But there was a tug in my chest I couldn't ignore, the kind that says something isn't finished yet.

I returned to Kuwait in that lull between holidays, just before the year gave way. The airport was hushed. The roads were half-empty. Even the city seemed to exhale.

I unpacked slowly, reacquainting myself with the familiarity of my space—the hum of the ceiling fan, the clean scent of my own shampoo in the bathroom, the blue couch waiting like an old friend. Nothing had changed. And yet, everything had.

On New Year's Eve, we made a plan.

First, dinner. A restaurant that tried hard to be elegant with heavy silverware, white tablecloths, polite candlelight. We talked about small things. Work. Travel. Food. We drank discreetly, as we always did. Beer disguised as iced tea, wine poured into water glasses. The usual choreography of life in a dry country.

He looked good that night. Understated. His sleeves rolled once, forearms sun-kissed from the desert. Not trying. Just present.

Later, we returned to my apartment. I lit some candles, some tall, some short, their flames flickering in glass votives along the bookshelf and windowsill. The room glowed with restrained intention, like it was waiting for something to begin.

I asked if he liked music. He shrugged. "Only if it's genuine."

So I played something simple. Classical. When the music changed, he stood and offered his hand. No performance, no grin. Just an open gesture.

I took it.

We waltzed into the new century. Not tightly. Not in a practiced way. The two of us, barefoot on the tiled floor, turning slowly in the candlelight. Where we come from, waltzing into the New Year is tradition, a gentle ritual to ease into what comes next. But this felt different. Like something opening. Like possibility.

Outside, the city made its own music—a scatter of fireworks, a few horns, the occasional shout from a distant balcony. Inside, it was quiet. Still.

And then it was midnight. He let go long enough to reach for our glasses. We clinked them gently.

"Happy New Year," he said, his voice low and certain.

"Happy New Year," I said back.

We didn't kiss. That would come later. But we stood close, glasses in hand, slightly out of breath. And for a long moment, we didn't speak. There was no need.

I wasn't nervous. I didn't scramble for words to soften the quiet. Instead, I felt present—anchored, awake in a way I hadn't been in years. And that's when I began to see him for what he was. He never reached for what wasn't freely given. He never pressed for what wasn't his to take. And something in me, a part I hadn't even known was clenched, finally let go. A long, slow exhale I'd been waiting for without realizing it.

The days that followed moved slowly, not painfully, but in a wintering way. Kuwait doesn't do January the way we do back home: no twinkling lights, no sales, no post-holiday crash. The city stays still, holding its breath for spring, when color and celebration will return to the streets.

December had emptied the place out—diplomats, aid workers, embassy staff. Gone home for family and familiarity. I had done the same. And now, back in this pause between years, quiet hangs over everything. Lighter. As if the season has finally stepped aside, just long enough for something else to be heard. I welcomed it. The hush made space for reflection. And, unexpectedly, for connection.

Nick had returned to his post, far from Kuwait City, stationed somewhere anonymous and windblown, where duty took precedence over comfort and the days blurred together. But the phone calls began. At first, brief. Just checking in. A comment about New Year's, a half-joke about the food on base. A question about a dinner we'd both missed.

But then they lengthened. Fifteen minutes turned to forty. Forty turned to ninety. I began to recognize his voice not just in sound, but in rhythm—the way he dropped the pitch slightly when he was unsure, the half-laugh that followed most of his stories, the steadiness in how he listened.

The connection was often poor. Background static, dropped lines, the echo of desert wind cutting across syllables. Yet, he called. Always. Sometimes twice in one day.

And gradually, a ritual emerged. The phone became our place, a strange, disembodied room where trust could stretch its legs. He told me about his medical studies, his long nights, the things he missed from home. And about the women before me, briefly, without bitterness. There was history there, but no heaviness. No need to prove or hide. Just truth, offered plainly.

I listened. And then, slowly, I began to speak.

I didn't open up all at once. That's never been my way. I don't hand over the past like a box of facts to be sorted through. I offer it in layers. In tone, in pause, in what I choose to say and what I let echo between the words. I started by telling him there had been someone. That it had mattered. That it had left its mark.

I didn't try to explain the shape of the relationship, not yet. I didn't want to say affair. I didn't want to say married. Not because I was hiding, but because those words—even in our own language, but especially in English—feel loaded. Flattened. Stripped of everything that made it real. I've had affairs before; I know their edges, their hollowness. What Marc and I shared was nothing like that. To call it an affair would make it sound banal, when in truth it had undone me, remade me.

Instead, I told him how it had felt. That it was powerful. Transformative. That the end had hurt—deeply. That I wasn't over it in the way people expect you to be after a year, or two, or ten.

And then one evening—a tender one—I said the name.

He didn't interrupt.

There was a faint sound of a breeze on his end of the line, brushing past the receiver. Somewhere in the distance, I heard a door creak, then close. I pictured him leaning against the edge of a metal desk, or maybe sitting on a low cot, one hand over the phone, the other resting on his knee. Still. Listening. Carefully.

They served in the same army. Not friends. Not enemies. But close enough for the name to land.

He didn't ask questions. He didn't draw comparisons. He didn't try to fold my story into his own. He just stayed quiet, not the heavy kind of quiet that demands to be filled, but a quiet that felt like space. When he finally spoke, it was simple, almost tender.

"Thank you for telling me."

It wasn't the words that stayed with me, but the hush that followed. The way he left the air uncluttered, as if he knew silence could cradle more than language ever could. It was the moment trust began to root—not through confessions or promises, but through the gentleness of being held without judgment.

With that, something shifted, almost imperceptibly. There were no grand displays or feelings of relief, just a subtle sense of being understood. I didn't feel forgiven; I felt seen. It dawned on me—perhaps for the first time—that this was a different kind of love, a different kind of man. Someone who could bear the whole of me, past and present, without hesitation.

After that conversation, there was a change between us. It wasn't dramatic—no proclamations, no grand shift in tone. Just a calm understanding that hadn't been there before. A sense of space that didn't need to be earned. A sort of safety I hadn't realized I was missing until it appeared: fragile at first, then fierce, then undeniable.

He didn't treat me differently. He didn't retreat. If anything, he became more consistent, not in grand gestures, but in the kind that actually matter. The calls kept coming. The questions grew softer. We began to speak less like people learning each other's details, and more like people who had already decided to stay.

In the weeks that followed, something began. We didn't name it at first. We just talked—on the phone, for hours, sometimes late into the night. His post was far away, in the desert, so the phone line was a lifeline. I would sit on my blue sofa, barefoot, a glass of wine in hand, the cord coiled around my fingers, and listen to the way his voice softened after midnight. Sometimes he'd call twice in one day. Once, even three times.

Eventually, someone at UN headquarters noticed. They sent a messenger to his observation point to check if the line had been compromised, as if the vulnerability was technical, not human. We laughed about it. But the truth was, it said something. We were no longer just talking. We were tethering.

And when the line fell silent, there were e-mails—the year 2000, when the novelty of that glowing inbox still felt like a secret window. His messages came like love notes: playful, tender, typed in the pauses of long desert shifts. I printed them out sometimes, just to hold the words in my hands, the ink smudging faintly beneath my fingertips.

I began to look forward to the sound of the phone. The way it would cut through the silence of my apartment, just as the day was winding down. I knew his rhythms. He learned mine. He told me stories from the field. I told him what I was cooking, what I was reading, what I was remembering.

Once, I heard the call being transferred, a patchy, low-tech handoff between military outposts. There was a delay in his voice. A moment of static. And then it cleared.

"Still there?" he asked.

"Still here," I said.

And that, strangely, was when I knew. Not in a rush of emotion. Not with tears or a racing heart. Just that phrase— *still here*—and what it meant. What it had come to mean.

It meant I wasn't waiting anymore. It meant he wasn't afraid of my story. It meant he wasn't trying to rewrite it. It meant he had already begun to love me, and I—without entirely meaning to—had begun to love him back.

Not in spite of everything. But with everything.

Our love blossomed swiftly, yet thoughtfully. Just under three weeks after New Year's Eve, we weren't merely spending time together; we were integrating our lives, aligning our plans, and discussing our future. He soon proposed, offering a genuine proposal with a ring and a question posed with a calm certainty, not from a place of impulsiveness, but because he was sure of his feelings. I accepted, not because I needed rescuing or was in a hurry, but because I had never been more certain about someone. Nothing about it was rushed; everything about it was perfect. We didn't stumble into marriage; we chose it—deliberately, completely, and without any doubt.

Redemption didn't arrive with fanfare. It came softly, as true things often do—calm, clear, unmistakable. It came through a man who didn't need perfection, who never asked me to erase what came before. He listened. He stayed. He made it safe to be fully known.

With Nick, I never had to explain why I was cautious or tender or hurting. I didn't have to shrink or translate my pain into something more palatable. I could be exact. And he would still be there.

There was no shadow in our love. No hiding. No performance. Truth wasn't a risk. It was the foundation.

So when the past resurfaced—when a familiar song played, when a ghost flickered through memory—I didn't retreat.

I remembered.

And I let it go.

Because I finally understood what love truly was. And it didn't hide.

I no longer lived in solitude, wondering whether a man would stay. I no longer measured my worth by how well I could carry someone else's secrets. I didn't disappear to earn love. I was seen. I was claimed. I was home.

We married the year we danced into. When I left Kuwait, I didn't walk into ease. Life got harder in many ways with another language, another country, another fight to build something from scratch. But this time, I wasn't doing it alone. We moved forward—not chasing what had been lost, but choosing what came next.

And in retrospect, I know now what I couldn't fully admit then: Marc and I were never built for forever. What we had was too intense, too fragile, too shaped by the impossibility of our circumstances. We were built for a summer.

Three United Nations peacekeepers crossed my life. The first was for fun. The second, Marc, broke me open. And the third, Nick, was mine to keep.

And that was the difference—Marc was never mine, but Nick was.

Epilogue

The Return

Twenty-five years later, I stand by the window of the apartment I now call home, coffee mug in hand. Back home. My real home. And yet, even here, my story was still unfolding.

Ich erinnere mich an die Ruhe und Klarheit, die den Beginn mit Nick getragen haben. Nach Kuwait zog ich erneut um, diesmal in ein Land, das nahe genug lag, damit Nick mich oft besuchen konnte, während er zuhause sein Medizinstudium beendete. Wir waren schon verheiratet, auch wenn unser erstes Jahr getrennt verlief. Jeder von uns war noch damit beschäftigt, das frühere Leben zu ordnen — jenes Leben, das es gab, bevor wir einander begegneten. Es sollte eine Weile dauern, bis wir wirklich angekommen waren, bis die Entfernung etwas Beständigem wich. Aber selbst damals, selbst in der räumlichen Trennung, wusste ich, was wir aufbauten.

Als die Zeit reif war, fanden wir hinein in unser gemeinsames Leben. Wir packten unsere Sachen, tauschten die trockene und karge Wüstenlandschaft gegen die grüne und gebirgige Schönheit unseres Heimatlandes. Ich kehrte dem diplomatischen Leben den Rücken und begann, eine andere Art Zukunft aufzubauen — eine, die auf Präsenz beruhte und vom Lernen und Lehren geprägt war.

Nick begann im nahegelegenen Militärspital zu arbeiten, nur eine kurze Fahrt von dem Vorort entfernt, in dem wir unser Leben aufbauten. Ich fand neue Wege, meine Stimme zu nutzen, neue Routinen, die meinen Alltag strukturierten. Zuerst als Ehefrau. Dann als Mutter.

Das Tempo von allem veränderte sich. Keine Botschafts-empfänge mehr, keine dringenden Depeschen. Nur ruhige Morgen bei Kaffee, Spaziergänge im Park und das langsame, bewusste Schaffen von etwas Dauerhaftem.

My hair is still blond, still long, though streaked now with silver, catching the light differently these days, in a more muted, subdued way. But still mine. My body has changed, of course. Childbirth does that. So does time. So does healing.

Somewhere behind me, music begins to play. Not *Sommermorgen*—that one belonged to us. The soft soundtrack of long drives and sleepy mornings, of sunlight on borrowed time.

This one is mine. *Because You Loved Me.*

He never knew. I never told him. It wasn't part of our story back then, but it became the one that stayed. Not the song of what we did, but the song of what it meant.

Because he loved me, I learned to trust what I felt.

I had lost my faith—in myself, in men, in being chosen—and he gave it back to me without ever saying the words.

He stood by me, just long enough for me to stand tall.

I had his love. For a moment, I had it all.

I don't turn the music off. I don't shed tears. I stand there, letting it move through me like it always does. Not breaking me. Not anymore.

I chose silence. A quarter century of it. No letters, no calls, no deliberate meetings. I never reached out or asked the questions that lingered. I let him live his life, and I lived mine. But time has a strange way of loosening knots. Of softening what once burned.

It was pure coincidence that we lived in the same neighborhood, yet even then I kept my distance. Now and then, life conspired to place us in the same space, but I never let it become more than a fleeting acknowledgment or a polite hello. The silence was mine—any breaks in it belonged to chance, or to him.

The lyrics float up before the chorus even hits. And suddenly, I'm no longer in my apartment. I'm twenty-seven. The desert heat clings to my skin. And he's still there.

I remember not just the mornings, the trips, or the kisses in the car, but how he loved me. It was a calm love, given freely, as if he trusted I'd carry it forward. Maybe it's the song that triggers it, or perhaps it is just the passage of time, smoothing out the rough edges. Or maybe both.

Whatever it is, something within me eases. Twenty-five years later—and for the first time since the day I heard his voice for the last time—I decide to send him an email. For once, I am the one to open the door.

He responds within hours, with no hesitation—just warmth and recognition, as if the distance between us never really existed. We exchange phone numbers. Although we don't talk often, when we do, it's as though time has frozen. Our voices sound the same, and the pauses between our words are still comfortably familiar. And beneath it all, something quietly unspoken lingers. Not quite desire, but a memory, an awareness of what once was. A flicker, not a flame. Nothing has truly changed, and yet everything has.

When we finally agree to meet in person, I invite him over for lunch at my apartment. I see him—really see him—for the first time in decades, not just in passing. We exchange the customary double-cheek kiss, the polite ritual of reunions and retirements. But for a single breath, something shifts. This isn't how we used to greet each other. I shake it off before he notices. Maybe he does. Maybe he doesn't.

We sit at the table in my kitchen. I've made lunch, like I used to: simple dishes arranged with my usual care, not to impress, but to offer something sincere. The room feels almost invisible to me in its familiarity, the apartment I share with Nick and my child. But with him here, it tilts strangely, as if the past has pulled up a chair in the middle of my present.

Time makes itself known in the faintest ways: on our faces, in our postures, in the air that settles between us. Of course we both appear older. Fine lines fan from his eyes, but still the same blue that startled me the moment he introduced himself, assured and disarming, a thread that stitched the years together. More silver streaks through his hair now. His frame is leaner, his stance more deliberate than I remember— less the easy sway of youth, more the grounded calm of a man who has settled into himself. He seems hushed, either more relaxed than I remember or more at peace in his silence.

Then I realize he no longer smokes. Neither do I.

There's no ashtray between us, no flick of a lighter, no lazy spiral of smoke punctuating our pauses. Somewhere along the way, each of us let it go—no grand resolution, just time erasing habits once so familiar. I don't miss the cigarettes. I miss what they offered: the pause and the way smoke filled the void when words felt too dangerous. Back then, smoking was part ritual, part rebellion, a companion on nights when he wasn't there, a rhythm in the waiting. Now there is no waiting.

He smiles, a familiar sparkle lighting his face, a hint of mischief that takes me by surprise. Our conversation begins lightly, covering topics like work, travel, and our kids. Yet it's the pauses that speak volumes—natural, comfortable, never burdensome. That calm silence allows me to breathe deeply. Not with a cigarette in hand, but still: it's a release. Not of longing. Not of remorse. Just the simple comfort of seeing him again and knowing that whatever we were, whatever burdens we carried, I've come to terms with it. I feel complete now. Not waiting. Not falling apart. Just... present.

When lunch ends, there's no dramatic goodbye, just a lingering moment, the soft cadence of voices promising nothing more than the ease of "see you soon." And then the door closes, and I'm back in my kitchen, the chair where he sat still warm.

And now, from time to time, we go for long walks—two people who once belonged to each other, speaking softly about lives that unfolded apart. Sometimes our shoulders brush, and for a heartbeat, I remember everything. And I think—maybe he does too. I've never asked. I don't need to. But if I had to guess, I'd say I never left his heart and he never left mine. Not as longing. Just as truth.

He tells me about his acrimonious divorce, how his wife left him, how the family was torn apart. I grieve for him when he tells me about the breakdown, the loneliness, the suffering. There's a recognition between us, the kind that once held both comfort and concealment.

Still a Secret

He came over for lunch again last week. I cooked—nothing fancy, just something warm and familiar. Something I knew he'd like.

He sat at my kitchen table like no time had passed, like we were still in that apartment in Kuwait, two people pretending the world wasn't going to change everything.

And then he ate.

He didn't talk much, just dug in like always—fast, focused, like the food might disappear if he didn't get to it quickly enough.

I watched him, and I laughed.

Because Nick eats the exact same way. As if there's a war just off-stage and this might be his last good meal.

That kind of hunger—it doesn't leave a man. Uniform or no.

There was something strangely comforting in it, watching him eat. Like some part of him was still the same. And maybe some part of me, too.

And then his phone rang.

It was her. His girlfriend. Or partner. Whatever she is now.

He didn't say my name.

Didn't say where he was.

Just softened his voice and kept me invisible.

I noticed. And yeah—it stung.

Not like it used to. There were no tears. No drama. Just this little ache under my ribs. Because even now, all these years later, I'm still a secret.

The difference is, I tell Nick. Every time. I always tell him.

Not because I'm guilty—I'm not.

But because I don't live in the dark anymore.

I don't hide people I care about.

I don't disappear the past just to make the present more convenient.

There was a time I thought secrecy made something sacred. That what was hidden was somehow more real. I don't think that anymore. I was once the woman who disappeared herself. I'm not her now.

He still hides me.

I no longer hide him.

That's the difference.

And maybe—maybe that's enough.

He's no longer the man I once loved, not in the way I knew him. He's something else now. Not a partner. Not a possibility. Just the imprint of a past so vivid it still stirs when I least expect it: a song in a store, a scent in a crowd, a silence too loud to ignore.

We talk now and then. Brief exchanges that acknowledge what we were without reopening it. But I no longer search for him in the solitary moments. The past has settled into something softer now. When he crosses my mind—as he still does —I let the thought land. I let the ache rise. I don't push it away. But I don't reach for more. I carry what was. Not as longing. Not as regret. Just as something true I once held. And then, gently, I let it go.

The Reckoning

There's one memory I try not to revisit, but it always finds its way back.

The Letter

It arrived just before Christmas.

A brief message. One paragraph. No preamble. He told me he was going to be a father.

Back then, we hadn't spoken in a few months. I had made the cut —clean, deliberate, necessary.

Not out of anger, but to move forward. The silence had been my boundary. The letter breached it.

I didn't think he meant to. But still—he reached back in, unasked.

And for a moment, it pulled me under.

Not because I wanted him back.

But because the timing spoke louder than the words.

Because I did the math.

And realized the child had been conceived while he was still mine —or at least, while I still believed I was his.

For a while, he stayed gone. But silence had a way of cracking open when I least expected it.

Years later, sometime after I had given birth to my own child, he showed up at the apartment door. Unannounced. Standing there with that same calm expression, holding nothing, offering nothing—just words. Congratulations. Nothing more. But enough. I remember being surprised by how cool Nick was about it. No questions. No tension. Just a quiet, almost amused awareness, as if ghosts occasionally showed up with pleasantries, and you simply acknowledged them, let them speak, and closed the door.

And that's all it was. A ghost, returning briefly to its old coordinates. And then fading again.

Over the years that followed, he began appearing like a thread running beneath the surface of my life. Occasionally, I saw him at the bus stop. The first encounter, our children acted as a sort of barrier between us. He gave a nod, and I returned it. *Hi*, I greeted him. *How are you?* he replied courteously. We never extended the interaction, and I couldn't bring myself to do so. After each encounter, I felt oddly uneasy. I was unsure of how to act—should I ignore him? Engage in small talk? Pretend we were two vaguely familiar parents and nothing more? The boundaries were blurred, and the silence between us seemed loaded with unsaid words. In short, it was awkward.

Then there was that ski trip, the one where he and Nick crossed paths. Both of them were holding skis, each accompanied by a child. I wasn't there, but Nick recounted it to me later. *We said hello. That was it.* No drama unfolded, just a moment of acknowledgment. They had never been friends, but they understood their connection to one another.

Years later, I spotted Marc again—at the military hospital where Nick worked. He was on the other side of a glass door. Just a fleeting glimpse. A shadow. His presence. My breath caught before I even realized why, my heart fluttering in that old, familiar way.

For an instant, memory tried to pull me back—heat on my skin, his impossible blue eyes, the echo of a love that once consumed me. But before it could take hold, I turned toward Nick, standing beside me, fully absorbed in a discussion with a group of doctors. Calm. Assured. Exactly himself. And in that moment, I reached for his hand. I needed to feel it, not just as an idea or a promise, but as something real and tangible: the warmth of his hand in mine, the grounded strength of his presence, the constancy I had once thought impossible."

There was no hesitation. No pain. No tug toward the past. Just this: the solidity of our life. The essence of safety. The feeling of home.

Still, I was taken aback by how easily memories could resurface. How a single look, a brief moment, a trace of him could bring back something I thought was locked away for good. Marc didn't own me. Not my time. Not my loyalty. Not my desires. And yet—if I was honest—he still existed somewhere within me. Not as a fire. Not even as a ghost. Just a shadow I had learned to live with.

Like an old cigarette habit—long quit, but still missed. I don't crave the smoke. I crave the memory of the smoke. The ease it gave me before I understood the damage.

There are days I still want to see him. Not to rekindle anything. Not to be touched or told I'm missed. Just... to feel that flicker again. That electric current of being seen in a way I once needed.

It's not love anymore. It's something else—unnamed, but familiar. Like the ghost of smoke you catch in the wind and turn toward before you remember you've quit.

What I Carry

In my life, I loved twice.

The first was a secret flame, bright and all-consuming, unfolding behind closed doors and within stolen hours. The second was an open embrace, slower and steadier, wrapped in honesty, built not on urgency but on trust. One love shattered me entirely, breaking something open that had long been hidden. The other held me with unwavering strength, meeting me in that brokenness and never asking me to hide again.

Marc was the wildfire—sudden, disarming, unforgettable. He entered my life like heat pressed against fragile glass, without caution, without hesitation, without apology. He never stopped to consider the cost. He simply moved, reckless in his certainty, and impossible to stop. He saw me, and in that seeing, sparked something alive in me I hadn't even realized was dormant.

Loving him was like learning a new language, one I didn't know I was fluent in until I spoke it with him. It wasn't safe, and it wasn't supposed to be. It was a love that asked for everything while offering nothing in return. And still I surrendered, because the sheer intensity of it made the world vanish around us.

Nick came into my life in a different way—softly and without any fuss. There was no dramatic spark or intense rush, unlike with Marc. With Marc, it was immediate, a burst, a consuming fire. But with Nick, it was different. Our romance moved quickly, yet without that explosive moment. Instead, there was an understanding, an unspoken mutual acknowledgment that we were meant for each other. He didn't ask me to forget the past or shy away from the truth. He stayed. With him, I opened up completely. I wasn't a woman in need of saving—I was simply a woman wanting to be known. And I was loved.

I carry both loves still, not as wounds and not as measures, but as pieces of my truth. One revealed the depths of what I could feel. The other revealed the strength of who I could become. They were never the same, nor were they ever meant to be. Not all loves are meant to last forever. Some leave a mark. Others remain.

Marc didn't stay. But he gave me something I hadn't had before: the unfiltered experience of being wanted, chosen, seen. He never said it, but in loving me the way he did, he was preparing me for the kind of love I would one day be ready to live. He taught me what love could be, long before I was ready to live it. Because he loved me, I learned how to receive love. How to return it. How to recognize it when it finally came to stay.

We never said "You and I, forever."

But in those moments, it was easy to believe we already were.

Our forever lasted a single summer.

The summer of 1998.

And so, as I close this chapter, I carry the lessons both men gave me—the fire, the stillness, the ache, the healing. I carry the woman I became in their presence. I carry the love that opened me, and the love that stayed when the opening was complete.

Because both were true.

I didn't plan for it.

I didn't expect it.

But I was deeply loved—once by the man who lit the match, and again by the man who kept the flame alive.

Acknowledgments

Every story is carried not just by the writer, but by those who stand quietly behind it.

To Marc—thank you for the memories that made this story possible. Without them, there would be no *First and Last Love* to tell.

To Julia, my editor—your insight, rigor, and care have been invaluable. You shaped these pages with a steady hand and made them stronger than I ever could have alone.

To KS—for walking beside me from the very first page, for sharing both the tears that fell over heartbreak and the laughter that spilled over the lighter moments.

To HRC—for saving my booty once again.

To my beta readers—for your honesty, your encouragement, and your trust. You helped me see both the flaws and the beauty in this work.

To my family—and especially to Nick, my last love—for your patience and your support, especially when this process grew heavy. You reminded me that writing is never done alone.

And to every reader who picks up *The First and Last Love*: thank you for stepping into this journey. May it stay with you, not as a secret, but as a reminder of what love, in all its forms, leaves behind.

A Note from the Author

The First and Last Love is not the end of my writing—only the beginning. There are more stories waiting to be told. Some have already found their way onto a page, others still live inside me.

If you would like to stay close to this journey—to know when new stories are released and to glimpse behind the curtain of the writing life—you can find me on Instagram: @frieda.shan.author.

And if this story touched you, even in a small way, I would be deeply grateful if you left a review on Amazon. Your words help other readers discover the book and keep me writing the next ones.

Thank you for walking with me through this one. I hope you'll stay for the ones still to come.

Frieda

Bonus Chapter

This story doesn't end here. I've prepared a bonus chapter —a piece that belongs beyond the last page. You'll also find a preview of my next book, *Captive Hearts* (working title).

Simply scan the code below to read it:

Thank you for being part of this journey.

www.ingramcontent.com/pod-product-compliance
Lightning Source LLC
Chambersburg PA
CBHW050340110726

47899CB00007B/2582